SPY FOR BROTHERHOOD

No. 7

B.E. WARE

FROM THE AUTHOR,
B.E. WARE

To the followers of the Hebrew scriptures and the biblical testaments of Jesus Christ and listeners of the revelations of Mohammad. To Brahmas, searchers of the divine reality in Hinduism and the seekers of enlightenment brought by Gautama Siddhartha, The Buddha. To the readers of the philosophy of Confucius, people of the planet Earth, and most of all the brothers on the street corner. This is an adventure story for you.

You may not believe what you are about to read, yet there are documents to substantiate ninety percent of what is contained within these pages. Four percent has been based on personal memory, 3 percent is the probability of an outcome, and another 3 percent is the desire of the author to bring you a readable story without straying far from the truth.

A release of liability was obtained from the real, living individuals who are portrayed in this novel. Over time, many of these individuals have since passed away. But, if there is anyone mentioned within who is still among the living who disagrees with what I have said concerning them, they are free to arrange polygraph tests (for both of us) dealing with this material. The names, dates, and places have not been changed.

Why?

Because, as members of the human race, none of us are innocent of the things found within these pages. Taken from the fifth book of Moses called Deuteronomy 15:9 (KJV), "Beware that there be not a thought in thy wicked heart, saying, The seventh year, the year of release is at hand; and thine eye be evil against thy poor brother, and thou givest him naught, and he cry unto the Lord against thee, and it be sin unto thee."

DEDICATED TO:

The seven million veterans of the Vietnam War 1954 –

1974

The late Master William Seven

And the American music industry.

B.E. WARE

The computer, a system based on components necessary in the processing of captured information, is based on the organic human brain that also captures, stores, and processes information. I will seek to use my personal storage device, the "memory bank" within my organic human brain, to display the information you will find in this story that was set to pen and paper in the year of our Lord, 1977.

Memory Bank Information Date: 1-7-1977
Time: 11:35 a.m.
Place: Apollo Village Apartment
Complex, Milwaukee, Wisconsin
Incident: Telephone Conversation
Subject Matter: Acknowledgment to
proceed with the literary manuscript.

The phone rings, and I answer. "Hello."

"Hello, is this three-two-five? I'm trying to reach out and touch a brother."

These are the last three numerals of my telephone number, letting me know the caller is from an organization known as "The Brotherhood of Men," and a coded message is to follow.

"Hey, brother man, how are you doing?"

"Everything's sharp blood, no sweat. I've got that information for you. Your father says it's okay with him if you use his name when you apply for the loan, just as long as you make sure there are no errors in the paperwork."

Interpretation: I have been given permission from the council of elders to write this novel.

The caller continues, "I also have some personal information your father felt may aid you in filling out the paperwork on the loan. I'll send it to you in the mail. He also requests that you return the document as soon as possible."

"Okay, blood, I'll check out the information when it gets here. Thank the old man for me when you see him, and tell him I'll have the papers back to him ASAP."

"Will do. Talk to you later."

On January 7, 1977, at 12:00 noon, I began to meditate and study the data I'd already compiled. On January 11, 1977, at 12:10 P.M., I received a plain manilla envelope in the mail containing events that had been previously unknown to me. On January 14, 1977, at 7:07 A.M., after seven days of fasting, praying, and meditation, I began to write this novel.

Memory Bank Activated: 1-14-1977
Content: Previously Unknown Data Covering
the Period Prior to the Year 1949.
Documents Received: 1-11-1977
Subject Matter: My Parents
Period: Seven Years Prior to my Birth, August
1942
Location: Small farm leased to Acie Ware (a
Black sharecropper) in the rural part of
Indianola County, Mississippi.

Two well-dressed Black men (names censored) are standing in a grove of trees that line the plowed field where a crop of cotton is being harvested. One is a professor of history who has an insatiable appetite for the science of genetics. He is from Jackson State University. The other is an instructor at Mt. Everett High School in the county of Mound Bayou. (Both belong to a newly formed group called The Brotherhood of Men.)

They seem out of place wearing suits. Muggy, suffocating heat had come with the hot August sun. The heavier of the two men loosened the knot of his tie, wishing he'd worn the light beige suit instead of the dark blue one. It is soaking up the sun like a sponge. Sweat pours down his back and under his armpits. He'd give anything to be back in his office at the university campus. Then, as if in answer to his wish, the other man raises his finger and points to the small group of people coming into the open field from the other side of the clearing.

"Look, there they are. That's them!"

Not wanting to be seen by the approaching newcomers, they step farther into the ring of trees. The professor takes the binoculars that are strung around his neck and raises them to his eyes. As soon as he takes a look at the two he came to see he can return to more comfortable surroundings.

The slimmer man directs him to the people they are concerned with. "He's on the left." He points. "And she's the second from the right."

The professor speaks without taking the binoculars from his eyes. "The male, what are the facts we have on him?"

Taking a notepad from his suit coat pocket, the other man thumbs through the pages. "Here it is." He reads from his notes:

"Name: J. T. Ware. At present, he is twenty years old and attending Utican Institute, a local agricultural school. From what we've been able to find out, he has an unusually high aptitude for learning complicated material and leans heavily toward mechanics and technical subjects."

Letting the glasses fall from his eyes, the professor sinks down to the base of the tree, propping his back against the large tree trunk. "What is his numerology?" he asks.

Turning more pages in the small book, the high school instructor sits cross-legged on the ground. "He's under the sign of Aquarius, born February 8,1922. Broken down, that's the second month, on the eighth day, that's plus one day, with the years adding up to our needs of three sevens plus one. As far as we can tell, he's one of the most likely candidates. His numbers are in proportion with the time sequence you worked out for us, and his genealogical trace shows that he could possibly be one of the descendants of the line of prophets. It's difficult to tell with records of African slaves being what they are. We can only guess as to the credibility of his being descended from this particular ancestry. But out of the twenty people we've found, he seems to be one of the most promising."

"And the girl?"

The professor wanted to know about her. Reading from his notepad again, the teacher gave him the information. "Her name is Ethel Lee Silas. She's a Cancer, born July

4,1924. That comes out the seventh month, the fourth day in the year of the four sixes." Closing the notebook, he stares out into the open field, watching the small group pick cotton.

"We arranged an introduction between them, via her brother Eddie who's been knowing the male, J. T., for some time. A romance of sorts has already begun to occur between them."

Turning to the other man, he asked the question that had been on his mind for some time. "Look, I know how important the Brotherhood is, but I still don't understand what our bringing all these people together to make babies has to do with the mission of the organization?"

The professor looks at him and smiles.

To break it down is complicated. It has to do with history, religion, genealogy, and the Black folks living here in America. Taking the biblical timetable, Revelations, and other forecasted events in the Bible, we added everything we could find historically connected with the so-called second coming of Christ. Checking the present situation of Black people in America, we're reasonably sure that they are the ones who will produce this "new ideology" that will free us from the grasp of the satanic mindset that has taken over the world. We believe this awaking needs to take place before there can be a return of a Jesus or a figure like him. That's why we are locating certain Black people here in America who may have roots that reach back to one or more of the prophets. This J. T. and the others can possibly be among the ones. If so, then we must make sure that they begin to reproduce as soon as possible. Time is running out. The devil is at his strongest and will be until we are well into the cycle of the dawning of the age of truth, commonly known as the Age of Aquarius."

The high school instructor was still at a loss. He spoke almost jokingly. "You mean we're looking for the parents of a messenger out here in a Mississippi cotton field?"

Turning over on his stomach, the professor raised the binoculars back to his eyes. A smile came to his heavy, dark face. *Yes, sir*, he thought to himself, not answering the other man's question. *That's exactly what we are doing.*

Memory Bank Activated: 1-14-1977
Subject: Previously Unknown Data
Year: 1949
Location: St. Louis, Missouri.

At the beginning of the Age of Aquarius, during the second month, on the day of the double sevens, in the year of the seven sevens, it came to pass.

Ethel looked out of her window. She could see the wind traveling like a small tornado, blowing puffs of debris across the lot behind the hospital. She guessed it acted like that because of the Kansas dust storms. Missouri wasn't far from Kansas if she remembered her high school geography. Maybe some of the little dust devils had gotten loose and were now playing outside her window. It was cold, colder than it had been for days.

Ethel looked at the thin layer of ice covering the leafless tree that reached the height of her second-story room. She shuddered, then realized she was inside the large brick complex, surrounded and cared for by the doctors and nurses who hurried past the door of her room. She'd heard somewhere that this particular hospital in St. Louis had been named after a Black man by the name of Homer G.

Phillips. Maybe that was why she'd chosen to have her child here instead of at St. Louis County Hospital

Childhood memories and thoughts of her mother came with the pride in being Black. It had seemed so out of place in the town of Shaw, Mississippi. Hearing her mother speak of Black accomplishments, she could still hear her favorite statement, used when she became very frustrated.

"Lord knows we as a people going to have to start sticking together."

Remembering Mississippi in the late 1920s and early 1930s, there had been little sticking together between Black people living in the small Southern town. Seems as if people were always fighting and cussing each other out. Her mother said it was because of being poor all the time, not just some of the time, but all the time.

"Poor." She'd say the word like it was an entity unto itself; made people mean and evil, keeping them fighting over small amounts of money and petty things. This hurt Black people more than anything, according to her mother's thinking.

She'd say, *The thing we had to overcome in our minds was the idea that life stopped for us because we were poor. You still have the potential to become anything you want to with applied ability and faith in God.*

Ethel shuddered again. She sat propped up in bed, looking out at the frozen, bleak scenery that was framed by the window of the sterile white room. Maybe that was what made her cold. The similarity between the white, snowy, ice-covered river flowing in the back of the hospital building and her white sterile room had given her the mental impression of being out in the cold. She would have to have someone close the curtains for her, she thought, then decided against it; that would block out the sun. If the scenery continued to bother her, she would just have to have them move the bed while still keeping it where she could look out of the window periodically. Anyway, she had to be careful of drafts and things. She'd just given birth to her third child, a boy.

Momma would be pleased, she thought, *to hear that one of her grandchildren had been born in a hospital named for a Black man, her coming from Shaw and all, which was a part of Mt. Bayou, Mississippi, one of the first all-Black American communities in this country. Maybe that was why my momma was so proud of being Black*, Ethel thought, *and living there in Shaw.*

She spent the next two days gazing out the window, watching the icy winds blow bits of litter and snow that reminded her of the Kansas dust devils she had seen in a western movie a few days earlier. Remembering how strange that night had been gave way to the new feeling of continually being watched. Joe, her husband, even made a comment about total strangers being unusually nice to him, giving them free tickets to the movies. At the theater, an elderly Black man offered to buy them popcorn. Things had happened like that since her pregnancy began. Another time, she recalled having this strange feeling was when she and Joe had first been introduced to each other, and again when she gave birth to their first child, Leroy. There'd been the feeling of being watched.

They'd gotten married, and she was expected just before Joe was drafted into the army. He shipped out with a Black unit, bound for the European theater of war a couple of months before the baby was born. When the fighting in Europe had ended, she'd thought Joe would be among the thousands of G.I.'s returning from the conflict with Germany. However, this was not the case. His company was reassigned, along with other special Black units, to an outfit fighting in the Pacific.

That was the way it was during the closing days of the Second World War. While the majority of the white troops headed home to their jobs and families after leaving Europe in early 1945, Black soldiers from that theatre were shipped to the Pacific (without the benefit of leave) to help with the coming invasion of Japan. Waiting to ship out, they got the news: a new type of weapon had been used against the Japanese, the atomic bomb. The war was over. He was put on a boat heading back to the States.

When he'd first gotten home, Ethel had been able to detect the bitterness he carried around inside. Then, after four or five months, he began to relax and turned his attention toward the future. They made preparations to move further north, to St. Louis, Missouri.

This was delayed by an illness suffered by Joe's father, causing him to postpone the trip until he had helped his younger brother, Fred, get in the crops yielded by the small farm. The short delay turned into a year. During this time, Ethel gave birth to her second child, a girl, whom they named Delores.

While Joe made arrangements for the trip north, Ethel recovered at her mother's house. Memories of Josie chasing the next-door neighbors' kids from her side of the "shotgun-style" side-by-side house brought a chuckle to her lips. The kids had a habit of creeping into Ethel's bedroom to steal a peep at the newborn baby. Like all kids, they eventually caused too much noise, bringing the wrath of her mother down on their heads. Thinking of the house enhanced the longing she was developing for the warm Southern weather and the company of her mother. No matter, she would see Josie soon and feel the burning sun's rays on her skin.

The sound of the opening door broke the spell that watching the swirling winds had put her in. She looked up; it was a nurse pushing a medicine cart. Looking at the things on the cart, she thought about the "white" fixation they had at the hospital. The cart, towels, cups, and even the pills she took twice a day were white. Ethel looked at the nurse's white uniform and burst out laughing. Not knowing what to make of the way her patient was acting, the nurse dismissed it as an aftereffect of giving birth. She turned to her chart that was clipped to the cart and started dispensing the correct dosage of medication.

Ethel decided that explaining her outburst to the nurse was too much of a bother. Taking the medication, she lay back, relaxing in the bed, waiting for the drugs to take effect. *Anyway*, she thought, *Joe is picking me up in a few hours*. It would be good to get out of the sterile surroundings. She looked back out the window, thinking once again how much she missed the warm weather they enjoyed in the Mississippi Delta. Watching the dancing winds, she soon fell asleep.

A half-hour passed. Suddenly, Ethel opened her eyes. A nurse stood over her, holding a blue bundle. It was time for the baby's feeding.

"Here we are!" the young lady cooed. "Take good care of him; he's the nursery sweetheart being born on Valentine's Day!"

She placed the baby in the crook of Ethel's arm. "That's a special little Valentine's package you've got there," she said, giving her a wink while she straightened up the pillows Ethel had propped up at the head of the bed. Smiling, she left the room.

Ethel lay there, looking down at the bundle of blankets coving her child. *What* is *so special about this baby?* she thought. And why did the hospital staff have this "thing" about her baby? Everybody was being nice to her…too nice! They'd switched her from the ward to a private room, something they had been unable to afford, saying it wouldn't add any more to their bill. She was told not to worry; the cost was taken care of. Even the administration staff members came to her room to ask how she was doing. They treated her like she was some kind of celebrity.

After two days of this, she began to wonder about it all. The previous night had been the weirdest. The young Black doctor who delivered the baby came to her room, accompanied by a young lady. They stood around the bed for a few minutes. While the doctor asked the usual questions concerning her present state of health, Ethel noticed the look of fixation on the woman's face as she stared at the blankets that covered the baby.

"Can I take a little peek?" Not waiting for an answer, bending over the bed, she gently pulled the blanket from the front of the child's face. Remaining there, without speaking, she seemed frozen. The unnaturalness of her actions caused Ethel to become irritated. She began shifting her weight in the bed, becoming more uneasy the longer the woman stared. Finally, after a full minute, she decided to put a stop to the staring contest.

"I'm sorry," she said, "but it's time for his feeding."

Seeming to sense the anxiety their visit was causing, the doctor took the lady by the arm. Nodding to Ethel, he gently pulled her toward the door. The lady followed, walking like she was in a trance, mumbling to the doctor.

"Did you see it?" she asked. "There was a soft glow around his face!"

The doctor shook his head in acknowledgment as they quietly left the room.

For some reason, what the woman had said kept entering Ethel's mind. Some kind of glow surrounding her baby? She'd searched him from top to bottom and seen nothing. Something was wrong in this hospital that had been named for a Black man, something she was unable to put her finger on.

Well, no matter, she thought, drawing the infant closer to her as she lay in the bed, waiting for her husband to pick her up. Joe would be coming to take her home shortly; she wouldn't have to worry about the crazy folks that worked at this place. Once again, memories of her youth pushed the present from her mind and filled it with warm thoughts and a longing for her home, while outside, the icy February winds continued to blow against her windowpane.

Memory Bank Activated: 1-26-1977
Subject: Joshua Ware, February 1949
Location: St. Louis, Missouri

B. E. Ware! What kind of name is that for the boy? It sounds like some kind of warning, Joe thought to himself as he turned the black Chevrolet into the alleyway next to the city bus terminal, careful to avoid a broken soda bottle in the middle of the alley. The name for the new infant had been chosen by his sister Dorothy, who'd traveled three hundred and seventy-five miles from Chicago upon hearing of the baby's arrival. Joe had protested, insisting the initials be changed to a proper name. After much haggling, they finally settled on naming the boy Billy Earl.

Parking the car in front of the single-family dwelling that housed his family, Joe locked the door to the vehicle and took the groceries he'd just purchased into the gray wooden building. Ethel was busy in the bedroom, changing the baby's diapers.

She saw him enter but said nothing. He went into the kitchen and put the bags of food on the table. It had been like this since before the new child was born.

Something was bothering her, and he was unable to figure out what it was. He wondered if she'd found out about the two children he had fathered by other women. If that was it, then it might be better if it were out in the open. Going to the bedroom, he paused in the doorway, watching her change the baby. Noticing the irritated look on her face, he decided to bring up the subject of his other children at a later time.

Ethel finished drying the baby, then placed him between two pillows in the middle of the bed. She left the room without saying a word. Joe went over and sat on the edge of the bed; he started cuddling his new son. Everybody commented on how much the boy looked like him. He could see that the youngster had a slender build and, most likely, had inherited his short height. What was most striking was his face. For Joe, with his "baby face" features, it was like looking in the mirror.

He thought about his mother and father living on the farm outside of Sunflower, Mississippi. They hadn't seen the baby yet. His father was ill the majority of the time, making travel difficult for him. They just had to wait until the infant was old enough to "hit the highway."

"B. E. Ware." He said the name softly, shaking his head as he watched the baby drift off to sleep. What would life be like for a Black man in America with a name like that? They'd done the same thing to him, given him the initials J. T. instead of a proper name. Later in life, on his twenty-first birthday, he'd chosen his own name.

The weather in Mississippi had been unusually warm that February day in 1943. Along with his mother, father, and pregnant wife, Ethel, he'd chosen his own name that day as the family gathered on the porch of the farmhouse to bid him goodbye. He'd been drafted into the army and was going off to war.

The picking of the name turned into somewhat of an ordeal. There'd been a great deal of astonishment when he chose the names, Joshua Titus, taking both names from scriptures in the Bible to replace the two single letters he'd been given. *Most people don't realize the importance of one's name*, he thought. He'd asked that his first son, who was born that April, just as he was finishing bootcamp, be given the name Leroy, after a favorite uncle in the family.

Looking at this new sleeping child, he was glad he'd insisted on the name change. Growing up Black in America and being poor was going to be tough enough to deal with, without a name that sounded like a warning from the Almighty.

Yet, during it all, he felt, for some reason, that the name he had wanted to change was the one God had intended for his son to have. Flopping back on the foot of the bed, he stared up at the ceiling, contemplating the future of his child.

Memory Bank Activated: 2-3-1977
Subject: My Personal Memory Data
Content: Period, Early 1950s

I fell to Earth at three. Along with me came the burning desire for communication with the world around me and a love of travel. My previous existence and this one left a number of unshakable impressions on my mind. A strong one was the fact that I was returning to this place and starting over. I had been here before.

At the age of two years old, I asked my brother and sister to teach me how to write my name so I would know who I was this time around.

My father, whom we called Joe, purchased one of the three-foot-high wooden boxes that housed a light green glass tube. They told me to call it a television. I wanted to take it apart; Joe stopped me. He and Ethel both insisted I call them mom and dad instead of using their first names. I told them I would if they let me go to live with my Aunt Dot in Chicago. Sometimes, Dorothy, who we called "Aunt Dot," came down to St. Louis on the train. Whenever we kids caught Ethel in a good mood, we'd have Aunt Dot persuade her to let us stay with her and Uncle John in Chicago. She'd ask to take us all, but she always looked at me when she did the asking. By the time I was five years old, I had done a fair amount of traveling to cities in the Midwest, with a couple of trips to Chicago and an unexpected visit to my parents' home in Mississippi. It was the 1950s and America was becoming the first world superpower. Everything was bigger and better than in any other country in the world.

There were millions of things I had to learn about. My mind told me that with my aunt Dorothy, I'd have a chance to learn about all the things I hungered to know. The chance never came. Joe and Ethel decided to get a divorce.

It happened the summer of my first vacation from grade school. Aunt Dot came down for a visit at the end of the school year, taking me and Delores back to Chicago for the summer. Leroy stayed in St. Louis with Joe. When we returned, just before the fall semester, things were not quite the same between Joe and Ethel. Without bothering to unpack our suitcases, Ethel loaded us aboard a southbound train headed for Mississippi. We stayed there with Grandmother Josie for a year while the paperwork that came with the divorce was being processed.

During that time, I had a chance to learn something about country life and meet the vast number of relatives who had remained in the Mississippi Delta region. One of the things that struck me as peculiar was the way everybody who lived in the immediate area had a note of pride in their voice when the name of the town, "Mound Bayou," was mentioned in a conversation. It wasn't until years later that I found out that Mound Bayou and the tiny suburb of Shaw, Mississippi, were one of the first all-Black communities in the country. It became easier to understand why Grandmother Josie was proud of being black and living there.

Memory Bank Activated: 2-9-1977
Subject: Chicago, Illinois, Mid-1950s
Content: Baptismal of Street Hustling

We'd lived in Shaw for nearly a year when Ethel found out she was pregnant. She'd been having an affair with the son of one of grandmother's neighbors. For reasons undisclosed to us children, they decided not to get married. It was possibly due to the fact that Ethel's divorce was not final yet. She announced shortly after finding out her condition that we were moving to Chicago, Illinois, with her brother, our Uncle Eddie, who'd come to pay Grandmother Josie a visit. Ethel hitched a ride for us on his return trip to the Windy City.

The first thing to hit me that autumn morning when we pulled into Chicago was the endless rows of brownstone apartment buildings stretching across the landscape. They gave the lower rent district of the city a shadowy appearance. It was in these gray sunless streets that I would spend my adolescence.

In the beginning, we stayed with Ethel's sister, Rosie, who lived with her husband and a growing family in a two-bedroom flat on Karlov Street, located on the west side of Chicago. It was while we were sharing those cramped quarters that on August 5, 1957, Ethel gave birth to her fourth child. She named him Reotha.

Not long afterward, we moved into another brownstone building a block down the street. This was the home of Uncle Eddie and his wife, Ollie May. The arrangement left us with nine people living in five rooms, counting my uncle's three kids. It took Ethel three months of pinching off her welfare checks to save the money needed to move into a place of our own. Meanwhile, I'd been learning about the dos and don'ts of the neighborhood from Uncle Eddie's oldest son, named after his father. Everybody called him Junior.

Aunt Ollie May gave Junior instructions to make sure he was with me every place I'd go. Understanding why this was necessary became clear about a week after we'd moved in with them. Junior and I had been sent down the street to pick up a mixing bowl that Aunt Ollie had lent to Aunt Rosie. Once on the street, the errand turned into a foot race.

Like all normal kids, we were forever trying to see who could run faster, jump higher, or hold their breath the longest. Without waiting for the starting countdown, Junior jumped the gun, running full speed down the narrow sidewalk. I took out after him, nearly catching up, when suddenly, three boys appeared out of one of the gangways in front of us. One of them stuck his leg out, causing Junior to trip headlong into the wire mesh fence surrounding the barren patch of dirt on which the city had been trying to grow a few blades of grass. He went down hard.

I winced at the impact of his bouncing off the fence and hitting the concrete. He cussed, jumping to his feet. I got ready for the fight I knew was coming. That was when the rest of the gang stepped out of the darkened walkway. There were maybe twelve or more. Some had names or catchy sayings like "Slick Rick" written on the waist-length cotton jackets a few of them were wearing.

The boy who had tripped Junior became the object of his friends' teasing remarks. One of the two who first appeared with him was the most sarcastic. Turning to him, the smaller boy poked him in the shoulder.

"Say! I know you going to kick this nigger's ass for running into you that way!"

At first, the big kid stood hovering over us, looking like he was unable to understand what was happening. Junior didn't wait to see if he planned on taking his friend's advice. He turned to make a getaway and ran smack into me, knocking us both to the ground.

The next thing I knew, the gang members descended on us like a ton of bricks. Forcing himself to his feet, Junior swung wildly at the group of boys. I grabbed an empty soda bottle that had been discarded on the ground. When I began wheeling the heavy piece of glass, the gang members backed away from us.

Taking advantage of their momentary retreat, Junior bolted for the safety of our apartment building back down the street. Following his lead, I threw the bottle into the crowd and lit out after him, hearing a sharp yell come from one of the boys behind me. The bottle had done some damage. I didn't bother to look and see what happened.

They came after us, giving chase all the way up to the back porch where they gathered, pounding on the kitchen door. Aunt Ollie May was the only adult at home at the time. Yelling through the door, she threatened to call the police. This did little to discourage them. Even if she called the cops, it would be some time before they arrived, if they came at all. The only way she got rid of them was by going to her bedroom closet and getting Uncle Eddie's hunting rifle. Once they saw through the window that she was armed, they left in a hurry, but not without threatening to bust our heads if they ran across Junior or me again.

I sat alone in the kitchen for an hour, thinking. The idea that something was wrong kept flashing in my brain. Was I in some kind of insane jungle made of concrete? If this was the norm around here, I thought, then I'd have to be on my guard from now on. Sitting on the top of the utility stool next to the refrigerator, I watched the kitchen grow dark from the fading sunlight. I wondered why I felt like I had existed before, in other times and places, and knew the ways of man, but this place was different.

**Memory Bank Activated: 2-18-1977
Subject Matter: Period: Fall 1957–
Summer 1959
Content: Personal Memory Data**

The second week in September, we moved into a five-room flat on the third floor of a storefront building located at 1400 Komensky Street, a block from both Eddie's and Rosie's families. Things happened fast during that time. Ethel was registering three of us kids in school, while also making the move and caring for our newly born baby brother. I became more independent, exploring my surroundings.

Most of the neighborhood kids attended Bryant Elementary School. Besides the everyday curriculum, I learned other needed subjects at the huge brick facility they called a school. My instructors were not employed by the school board, but their course of study was equally, if not more, important than the "three Rs." It was a course in street knowledge, and it came from my classmates. For instance, I learned that the West Side of Chicago was cut up into territories by street gangs. It didn't take me long to find out I lived in the street gang called the Egyptian Cobra's turf, one block from Pulaski Road, which acted as the dividing line between them and a rival gang called the Vice Lords.

If you lived on a gang's turf, it was automatically assumed that your sympathies lay in that direction. Most of the boys became gang members when they reached an age between twelve and fourteen. This gave me a few years before I would be confronted with the problem. I decided to make the most of the time by compiling as much street savvy as possible.

**Memory Bank Activated: 2-19-1977
Subject: Chicago, Illinois,1959
Content: Bitten by the Devil**

On June 28, 1959, at 10:00 o'clock in the morning, I was standing on the corner of 14th and Komensky with three friends, my next-door neighbor Ellis and the twins Tony and Terry, who lived a block down the street. School was out for the summer, and the four of us were hanging on the corner, looking for a way to get money for show fare to see a movie. The theater was air-conditioned, a great way to stay cool for a couple of hours. If you're ten years old and your mother is on welfare, you don't get much spending money.

Having lived in the upstairs apartment for two years, I'd learned to make it on my own as far as things like show fare, toys, or junk food were concerned. This was why the four of us hung out on the corner in front of the grocery store because a lot of people passed by going to make purchases, making it the best spot for a hustle. By helping people carry their groceries to their nearby houses, we could pick up a few coins. Pooling our monies together, sometimes we'd have enough to get everybody in the movies. This time, we came up a dollar and fifty-eight cents short. We were all bonded by our friendship to get the extra money. According to the code we lived by, without it, none of us could go to the movies. Tony came up with an idea.

"I know where we can get forty or fifty cents from. My mother has six or seven cartons of empty soda bottles…"

Ellis waved his hand in Tony's face. "That game is 'getting old," he said sarcastically. "You can run around collecting bottles if you want to. I got better things to do!"

Just then, a young boy came down the street, pulling a wagon made of an old orange crate. Because of the lack of funds, many kids had to make whatever toys they owned. We watched him stop at the corner, waiting for the traffic to lighten up so he could cross.

Seeing the wagon gave Tony another idea. "Say, why don't we go over by the large A & P grocery store? I've still got my wagon. Maybe we can make the money delivering groceries over there?"

Ellis didn't want to hear it, getting upset. "Come on, we ain't got time for that kind of game. I keep telling you! It could take hours to make the money doing that." A sly grin played on his face. "But there is one thing we can do."

Terry got into the act. "Yeah, and what's that?"

Ellis smiled. "Since we don't have time to make the money, let's take it."

Tony was puzzled. "Take it from where?"

"From who, stupid? From chumps like him!"

Ellis pointed at the boy with the makeshift wagon. He was heading for the A & P supermarket, located in the middle of the block on Pulaski Avenue. There were usually a half dozen kids hanging around the store, trying to make some spending change. Sometimes older boys would catch the smaller kids and take their hard-earned money, along with anything else they may have of value.

Tony shook his head. "I know what you mean, man, but if we get busted, it can cause a lot of trouble. I don't know if I want to get off into something like that!"

Ellis looked around at him. "You scared? That's what it is; you're scared!" He turned to Terry. "What about you? You like your brother here, scared of some delivery boys?"

He started laughing at them, forcing Terry to take the challenge.

"I'm not afraid! I ain't scared of nobody!"

Tony sat down on the steps to the store with a resigned look on his face. If his brother was in it, he had to go along with the hustle. Ellis knew he had them. He turned to me. "What about you, Billy? You in on this?"

I wanted to say no, which meant I'd become an outcast from the group. Feeling the pressure, I gave in. "Okay by me; whatever you guys want to do."

Ellis started off down the street toward Pulaski Avenue, with the rest of us close behind. Stopping at the intersection of 14th and Pulaski, he motioned for us to stand in the doorway of the tavern occupying the southwest corner. From there, we had a good view of the front of the food store.

We counted only four wagons, waiting for someone who needed help with their bags of groceries, lined up against the wall under the big glass windows.

"Now, here's what we'll do." Ellis gave us the plan. "Let's wait by the tavern next to the store until one of them takes an order, then on his way back, we'll jump him. That way, he should have some money on him."

About five minutes passed when suddenly, a wino came out of the tavern, almost crushing Terry behind the heavy wooden door. He was drunk and stinking to high heaven. The smell of cheap wine and his unwashed body were overpowering. I felt like throwing up. He got loud with us.

"What are you little niggers up to? You ain't old enough to come in here. Get the hell out from in front of this door before I call the owner out here to kick your little asses for you!"

Ellis, who was the taller of the four of us, stood up to him.

"You jive, filthy fink! You gonna get your ass kicked messing with us!"

The drunk hesitated, unsure how to handle the tough kid's retort. Ellis looked like he wanted to punch the old man in the mouth. It appeared like he was going to do just that when Tony tapped him on the shoulder.

"Look," he said, pointing across the street.

We saw two boys loading a customer's bags onto their wagons. We forgot about the wino and watched the boys helping the elderly Black woman with her goods. They finished loading the wagon and took off down the street. We followed. Terry stopped in the middle of the intersection. Turning back, he spat at the wino, who started cussing and gave us the finger. Terry picked up an empty wine bottle and threw it, causing him to duck back into the tavern.

The old lady lived four blocks from the store. Staying about a block behind, we watched them stop at one of the brownstone buildings. They had to come back our way in order to return to the store. Hiding in a gangway, we waited. It didn't take long. In a couple of minutes, the two boys came down the street, pulling the wagons. When they made it to the entrance of the gangway, we jumped out in front of them.

My mind was spinning! Everything seemed like it wasn't happening, like I was in a bad dream. A voice inside of my head kept saying, *You're not supposed to be doing this.* The whole scene reminded me of two years earlier when Junior and I'd had a confrontation with the gang members. Looking at the frightened expressions on the faces of the boys, I wanted to tell Ellis to call it off, but it was too late. Grabbing one of them, he went into a tough guy act.

"How much money did you get?"

Before the frightened boy could answer, Ellis was going through his pockets, taking the money he found, while Terry did the same to the other boy. Then he backed him up against the side of the building. Menacingly, he threatened him, "You ain't gonna tell nobody what happened, are you? Do you hear me? You don't tell nobody!" Then he hit him in the mouth.

The other boy ran down the street, yelling for help. Ellis took off running as fast as he could, with Tony and Terry behind him. I stood there for a few seconds, not sure about what I should do. Then something told me to get out of there or I'd get into a lot of trouble. Breaking the spell, I ran after the gang. My mind worked overtime as the realization hit me; I'd just been involved in a robbery. Small as it was, it was still a robbery! Not liking the feeling, I ran faster.

Memory Bank Activated: 3-6-1977
Subject: Chicago, Illinois, 1959
Content: Hoodlums of the Mind

"Billy! You want some popcorn? Hey, man, I'm talking to you!"

Terry elbowed me in the ribs, bringing me out of the daze I'd drifted into. We were in the movie theater over on Roosevelt Road, having used the money taken from the delivery boys to finance our trip to see the weekly serial that was playing on the screen.

I took a handful of the popcorn Terry offered me and tried to concentrate on the picture. It was no good. My mind kept slipping back to the robbery we'd committed, and oddly enough, I found myself thinking of something that had happened a week earlier.

***

The day had been exceedingly warm, and I had little desire to attend the choir rehearsal at the storefront church pastored by my aunt Rosie's husband, Uncle Nathaniel. Ethel insisted that my sister Delores and I join the junior choir, so there I was, standing on the sidewalk in front of the church, waiting for the auditions to start.

Melancholy and a desire to be someplace else produced a moment of gloomy reflection. This was aided by the deep dark clouds forming on the city's skyline.

"Ah, the wonders of the universe."

The stranger's voice startled me; my head jerked around to see who it was. I hadn't noticed the tall young man who had apparently been standing beside me for several seconds. I didn't say anything. Living in Chicago, you learn to keep your mouth shut and not get involved with people you don't know. He seemed to sense this, smiling openly, trying to ease my suspicions.

"Kind of funny how Allah sends the rains to cool off the Earth whenever that old sun gets to shining too brightly," he said.

His serene manner of speaking fascinated me. The only problem was that I'd never heard of this "Allah" he was referring to. Before I could ask who he was talking about, one of the deacons came out of the church. They greeted each other with a handshake I'd never seen before, undoubtedly having known one another for some time. At first, they stepped off a way, making it difficult to hear what they were saying. My curiously aroused, I moved closer to them.

Studying this smooth-talking stranger, I noticed how clean he was. Cleaner than any Black man I'd ever seen. Not in the flashy way the pimps and hustlers dressed, but more businesslike, more conservative. Even more unusual than his dress was what he was saying to the deacon.

"It's their minds, brother, it's their minds that we got to reach. That's where the trouble lies. Most of the kids today are hoodlums only in their minds. They aren't hardened criminals to be caged up and treated like animals. If we clean out their minds, we can put them on the right track. That's the only way to stop the gangs and the crime in the streets."

The deacon shook his head in agreement. What he was saying caused me to stop and think about Ellis and the fellows I hung around with. My mind related to what he was saying, to the things we did in the streets. For the first time, I was able to see how I was being manipulated by what others wanted me to do and not by what I knew was right.

What he said made a lot of sense, but I wanted to hear more. Unfortunately, one of the ladies from the choir came out of the church building; she began ushering the children inside. I was about to start for the door when the stranger stopped me.

"You've got a hard job ahead of you, young brother." Looking intensely into my eyes, he said, "It's up to you and your peers to bring into being a new age of enlightenment. Try to keep your mind clear and avoid the traps the devil sets in your path. Remember who you are and why you have been sent here." He tapped his index finger against his temple and said, "It's all in your mind, little brother."

Turning to the deacon, they shook hands again, and he started down the street, stopping here and there, talking to the people he met, trying to get them to buy one of the newspapers he was carrying. At first, it seemed funny, his selling the papers. As I watched him moving among the people, I realized he was selling more than a simple newspaper; he was selling an idea, and his words lingered in my ears as I filed into the church. I could hear him saying, "How about you? Got your *Mohammed Speaks* today, my brother? And you, sister, how are you doing today?"

***

Terry snapped his fingers in front of my face like he was bringing me out of a trance. "What up? Are you daydreaming or something?" He laughed. "Bet you can't even tell me what the movie was about. Come on, we're leaving."

We got up and moved toward the exit. Terry kept looking at me. "You aren't still scared, are you, about what we did?"

"No," I answered, pretending to get mad so he'd drop the subject. He wouldn't let it go, keeping after me as we walked out of the theater into the fading sunlight.

"Okay then, tell me what you were thinking about!"

I got loud with him. "You want to know what I was thinking about? The mind. I was thinking about the mind and how it works!"

Terry busted out laughing, unable to control himself. Ellis and Tony came out of the theater, sharing a box of popcorn.

"What's so funny?" Tony wanted to know what the joke was.

It took Terry a few seconds to collect himself. Pointing at me, he explained between giggles, "This nigger talking about he just spent four hours sitting in a movie thinking about the mind." Then he doubled over, laughing as hard as he could. Tony kind of smiled, still not sure what had Terry in stitches.

Ellis turned to me and said, "You are wasting your time, Billy."

Walking away, I could hear him softly say, "Niggers don't know anything about the mind."

I thought about the tall stranger. Too bad he wasn't around. Somehow, I had the feeling he knew about the mind. We started for home, keeping an eye out for other boys who would do to us what we'd done to the delivery boys a couple of hours earlier.

Memory Bank Activated: 3-8-1977
Subject: Chicago, Illinois, 1960-61
Content: The Little Red Wagon

It'd been a year and a half since the incident with the delivery boys. Now the tables were turned. I was the one walking the streets, pulling a little red wagon.

I'd been instructed by the juvenile courts to straighten up or be institutionalized. They put me on a year's probation because of an occurrence earlier that year. Ellis was responsible for what happened. He, Tony, and Terry isolated me from the group. They'd begun to emulate the older hustlers that hung out on the same corners as we did, only their street games were bigger and worse. The only things my friends were able to copy were their bad habits, like drinking wine and smoking cigarettes. When I started drifting away from the drinking, it caused a split between us.

One day, while returning home from the A & P store on Pulaski with Delores, Ellis was waiting for me, sitting on his front porch. Coming over, he stopped us at the bottom of the hallway leading to our upstairs apartment. Putting his arm around my shoulder, he said he wanted to talk to me for a second; Delores continued up the long flight of stairs. We'd taken about five steps toward Ellis's house when, without warning, he threw me to the ground and jumped on my chest, pinning my arms to the concrete.

I struggled to get free. Bending over me with his fist raised, he shouted, "Stay still, nigger, or I'll smash your face in!"

Delores heard the shouting, came back downstairs, and saw what was happening. She ran next door and yelled for Ellis's mother to come out and see what he was doing. When the door opened, he jumped off my chest. It was only one of his sisters at the door, but her coming made him release me. I got up, ready to fight. Delores's pleading was the only thing that stopped me. Ellis just stood there, laughing, while she pulled me back into the doorway of our building.

The next day, all hell broke loose. I'd spent the day in Franklin Park, where the neighborhood kids would go to play baseball or go swimming in the popular county park pool. Since carrying a weapon was the safest way to travel the half-mile from my house to the park, I'd carried my own bat to the softball game we'd played that morning. It was with me that afternoon when I returned home. Not wishing to carry it back into the house, I left it behind the downstairs hallway door while going inside the store for a soda. Forgetting it was there, I went upstairs to relax and watch some TV.

I wasn't in the house five minutes before Ethel wanted me to go back to the store. That was when the trouble started. When I got to the bottom of the stairs and flung the door open, Ellis and a young light-skinned boy named Ricky sat on the entranceway steps. Ellis had a mischievous grin on his face. Something was wrong. I felt a hassle coming on, and as the silence lingered in the air, I decided to make the first move.

"Say, can I get by here?"

Maybe they were just sitting on the steps because it was one of the few shady spots out of the hot autumn sun? I was wrong. Ricky looked at me with hate in his eyes.

"No, little jive-ass nigger, you ain't getting by here!"

This was hard to understand because we barely knew each other. I was unable to control myself, becoming madder by the second.

"Wait a minute, I live here! You know that don't you?" Anger made my voice shake.

Ricky clenched his teeth. "That don't cut no ice around here, sucker! If you want to get by, move me!"

My mind told me to keep calm. Ellis hadn't jumped into the conversation yet.

"Look, Ricky," I tried using persuasion on him, "I don't want to get into anything with you, but you're not going to stop me from leaving my own house!"

Rickey jumped to his feet. "Well, move me then, motherfucker! Go on, move me!" he shouted.

In his hand was a round, large stick I hadn't noticed it before. When he drew it back to swing at me, it got tangled in the row of mailboxes nailed against the outside walls. I jumped back into the hallway, trying to avoid the blow that never came. Seeing there was no room to swing the club, he jabbed at me with the jagged edge of the stick, hitting me above the right eye. Grabbing the door, I slammed it in his face, and losing his balance, he stumbled onto the sidewalk and fell. That was when I saw the bat I'd left behind the door only a few minutes earlier. Pulling the door open, I charged onto the sidewalk with the bat in my hand. The stick lay on the ground. When he saw me, he reached for the stick. About the same time he got his hands on it, I let him have it across the forehead with the bat. He grabbed his head, moaning and kicking. Blood squirted from between his fingers. Turning, I looked for Ellis, realizing he was probably responsible for what was happening. I wanted to give him the same treatment. He was nowhere to be found.

I ran upstairs, leaving Ricky lying on the sidewalk. Ethel wanted to know what was wrong and why I hadn't brought her the things she sent me to get from the store. She became upset, thinking I'd been goofing off instead of running the errand she'd sent me on.

The details of what happened didn't come out until an hour later when two detectives came to the house to arrest me. Ricky's parents had sworn out a battery complaint. Nothing either Ethel or I said, nor the wound above my eye, made any difference to them about who was attacked first. They took me to jail, and I spent the night in juvenile detention. The next morning, I was given a hearing date, assigned a probation officer, and released into Ethel's custody, still unable to figure out why I was the one being charged when I'd been the one attacked.

My probation officer was a black man who talked, dressed, and acted like he was a judge and jury all rolled into one. Ethel would take me down to the courthouse to keep the appointment dates he'd given us, but for some reason, he was never in his office. After three failed attempts to catch him in his office, we gave up trying. Within a couple of weeks, Ethel got a letter from the court saying she was to bring me in for a hearing.

When we went before the judge, what was said was a shock to both of us. This man had reported to the judge that Ethel refused to meet with him or keep the scheduled appointments. The judge threatened to discipline Ethel and confine me to the detention home. Her insistence that she had witnesses to prove she had brought me down to the probation office was the only thing that stopped him.

Instead, he put me on a year's probation, stating that I report once a month to the Hypocritical Black man with an authority complex. This was why I was pulling the little red wagon down the street, delivering newspapers. The probation officer had insisted that I "go straight" and find a part-time job to keep me off the streets.

So now, instead of being one of the "wolves," I was one of the lambs, waiting for the slaughter. The wolves finally took the bait. I was about a block from my house when they spotted me, two boys, both a couple of years older than me. Upon seeing them, I started to cross the street. They had a look about them that flashed a warning in my brain. I was too late; they also crossed over and walked right up to me, blocking my path. I was stopped in the middle of the block. One of them had his shirt off and tied around his waist. Reaching out, he grabbed me by the collar, balling his other hand into a fist.

"You the little bastard that jumped on my brother the other day, aren't you?"

He was lying, using the fake excuse to pick a fight and take whatever monies I'd collected on the paper route. I stood there, looking into his eyes, waiting for the blow to come. Suddenly, everything around us began to glow brighter and brighter and finally disappeared in a blaze of white light. At first, I became frightened, not knowing what was happening. Trying to move, I found I couldn't. This hadn't seemed to happen to my attacker. He continued talking. I could see his face and nothing else. His lips moved, but no sound came out. When he drew back to swing on me, everything went black.

Unable to move or see, I stayed that way for how long I'll never know. When my vision returned, I was still in the middle of the block. It all happened in the span of a few seconds. The kid who'd confronted me was down on his knees, holding his right eye. I didn't understand what was happening. Looking at the other boy, I saw a look of amazement on his face. He bent over his friend, trying to see the damage to his eye. I didn't wait to find out what had happened or give them another chance to jump me.

Bolting for the door to the apartment building, I pulled the wagon up the front steps and slammed the door a split second before the two boys got there. They remained outside, pounding on the door.

Ethel was visiting one of her friends who lived on the first floor. They heard the noise and came to the top of the first flight of stairs. She asked me what all the racket was about, and I told her. Coming down, opening the door, she faced the young men. The one who'd been hit shook his fist at me as I peered from behind her.

"I'm gonna get you, you bastard!" he screamed. His right eye was swollen and puffy.

Ethel put her hands on her hips and said, "Listen here, little nasty nigger! I don't want to ever see you around my house again, or I'll whip your nasty tail myself. Now get away from here before I call the police!"

They walked away mumbling, looking back periodically with hateful glances. After they were out of sight, Ethel turned on me. Hollering and yelling, she got on my case about always getting into trouble. If I kept it up, I'd have to leave her house. What she was saying didn't even register. I was still mesmerized by what had just happened. It was as if time and space had stopped, and someone stepped in and delivered the blow that had swollen the boy's eye. I felt like I'd been guarded against injury by some unknown force. It started me thinking about guardian angels and God.

Memory Bank Activated: 3-11-1977
Subject: Egyptian Cobras
Content: 1961, Initiation

The clock on top of the dresser read 9:58 P.M. I got out of bed and put my clothes on. The boys were coming to pick me up at 10:00 P.M., and I had to meet them downstairs in front of the store. Being extra careful not to wake Ethel, who was sleeping in the room next to mine, I slowly creeped out the door. It was late October 1961. A month before, I'd begun classes at a new school, Mason Upper-Grade Center. The guys who were waiting for me, for the most part, attended school there. We were meeting on this cool fall night to be initiated into a branch of the gang called the Egyptian Cobras.

Making for the back door, I opened it to find Matt Green, along with fourteen or fifteen other young boys, milling around, passing a bottle of White Port and Kool-Aid. Matt was a classmate of mine who lived on 16th Street, near the end of the westbound L-train, just before it crossed into Cicero County. This put him in the heart of Cobra territory, while I lived a block from the dividing line

(Pulaski Road) between the Cobras and their archenemies, The Vice Lords. Matt said this was why they wanted to check me out, to make sure I wasn't a Vice Lord.

All day long at school, whenever I'd pressure him about the initiation, he'd only say that you had to be tough to pass it. When my eyes became accustomed to the dim street lighting, I was able to make out a few faces in the crowd. Some were from school, and others lived in the neighborhood.

Without saying a word, Matt took off down the street, and the rest of us followed. It surprised me how quietly the large contingent moved through the dark deserted city streets. Every now and then someone would make a noise or raise their voice, immediately bringing a rebuttal from Matt, who reminded us we only had an hour before the 11:00 P.M. curfew and we didn't want the cops down on us.

Our destination was Franklin Park, one of the meeting places of the Cobras. Entering the ultra-bright light that beamed down on the baseball field, the guys went wild, playing like they were actually involved in a baseball game. They horsed around, sliding into home plate, and climbing up the wire mesh fence that serviced as a backstop for the batter's box.

Matt walked over to the team bench on the sidelines and sat down. Curious to know why we'd stopped in the park, I went over and asked him. He told me that a rendezvous with the chief warlord of the Cobras was supposed to take place. Ten minutes later, the park looked as if it were being invaded by an army on the march.

There must have been fifty or more teenagers climbing over the iron picket fence at the other end of the grassy field. Everybody stopped the horseplay and watched them coming toward us. We closed ranks, not sure if they were friendly or not. Sometimes, rival gangs roamed the neighborhood, looking for a rumble.

Matt put us at ease; he placed his fingers in between his teeth and let out a shrill whistle. One almost identical came back from the crowd that approached us. When they got close enough, I could see the Cobra snake head and fancy writing on the sweaters and jackets many of them were wearing.

They appeared to be the high school lettermen sweaters that the athletes wore around the school. The only difference was these read, "The Mighty Egyptian Cobras," with the nickname of the gang member sewn on in smaller letters. They surrounded us.

I recognized the leader immediately. He was an older boy named Morris who was in his last year at Mason. Later, I found out he'd been put back two semesters for not attending classes and being thought of as a general troublemaker. His younger brother, Marcellus, was in the same grade as Matt and me. He stood behind his brother as if waiting for a command to carry out his orders. Ignoring the rest of us, Morris took Matt aside.

At first, their conversation was unintelligible. Then Morris began raising his voice, sounding as if he were the meanest dude alive.

"Come on, Matt," he was saying, "I ain't got all night to be messing around with no little kids, man! If any of them got the guts to be a Cobra, stop wasting time, and let's get to it!"

Matt tried to calm him down. "Okay, but before we do that, I got something I want a couple of them to help me do."

Morris had a reputation around school for having a quick temper. It flared out of control. He started yelling, his facial muscles tightening.

"Say, look! Didn't I just tell you I had something jumping off in a few? We ain't got time for this bullshit!"

The nonchalant air Matt usually carried faded. He stepped away from Morris. A note of frustration entered his voice. "But we got to have some pieces. The other gangs have got guns! How are we supposed to defend our territory when they come over here looking for a rumble and they packing? That's all I'm saying. We need some pieces, and I know where we can get at least one."

Watching Morris, he waited for a reaction. After hesitating for a second or two, Morris spoke, sounding like he didn't believe him. "All right, show me this piece you talking about."

Instructing the rest of the gang to wait in the park, half a dozen of us followed Matt. Stopping a block from 16th Street, we turned into the alley. Hushing everybody, Matt warned us to remain as quiet as possible. Grabbing me by the arm, he pulled me close to him and whispered in my ear.

"You and me and Wayne are going to go in."

He pointed to the second floor of a tenement building not far from the corner of the alleyway. Wayne, who I'd met over at Matt's house, was a tall, thin, light-skinned boy we nicknamed Ghost because of his light skin coloring. He was already on his way up the darkened back stairs of the building. When Matt and I reached the second-story window, Wayne was running his hands along the windowsill, looking for a way into the apartment.

"I don't think anybody's home." he whispered.

Testing the latch on the window, he found it wasn't secure. Wayne gave it a good push upward with his fingertips, and it gave way. After making sure the noise hadn't aroused anyone, Matt helped him through the open windows. He unlocked the door and let us into the silent apartment.

Matt acted like he knew the place; he pointed, "Come on this way; it's in the bedroom closet."

When we got to the back of the house, he went straight to the bedroom closet door. Opening it, he pulled out a long leather case. Laying it on the bed, he unzipped it and pulled out the weapon, a shotgun. For some reason, I imagined it was a pistol we were after. The shotgun seemed out of place in the scheme of things. Putting it back in the black leather case, Matt turned to Wayne and gave him a push toward the closet.

"Get the shells. They're on top of the shelf."

Wayne ducked in and came out with two small square boxes. The grin on Matt's face was visible even in the dark.

"That's it," he said. "Let's get the hell out of here!"

We left the apartment, half running down the stairs. Reaching the bottom, Matt held up the leather case so everyone could see we'd made the score. Then, without a word, we took off at a slow trot, heading back to the park.

When we arrived, most of the other gang members had left. Morris had stayed. He was to meet them later. He took a look at the shotgun and nodded his approval, talked a few minutes alone with Matt, then told us he would see us tomorrow for the initiation ceremony. After he'd gone, we sat around admiring the beauty of the shotgun. It was brand new!

Wayne suggested it was easier to hide and carry if we sawed off the barrel and part of the stock. Matt agreed.

"But first," he said, "we got to figure out where to stash it for the night."

He looked around the crowd to see if there were any takers. Nobody offered to be responsible for the weapon.

Wayne spoke up. "Let's settle it this way. Whoever can use it the best gets to keep it for the gang."

"Say, that's cool!" one of the boys said. "So what do we shoot at?" Everybody began looking for a target.

"How about that?" Smiling, Matt pointed at a streetlight near the alleyway at the edge of the park. Wayne broke open a box of the shells and gave a handful to Matt, who fed them into the chamber of the twelve-gauge shotgun.

Walking to the mouth of the alley, we stood under the light while Matt gave the gun to Wayne, who put it to his shoulder and pointed the barrel at the pale glowing light. The noise of the blast was deafening, but the shot missed the lamp post entirely. Wayne cussed at having missed the shot. Matt took the shotgun and gave it to another boy, who also missed.

Then it was my turn. It was the first time I'd held any type of firearm. Adjusting my stance to accommodate the weight, I braced it against my shoulder, aimed at the light, and pulled the trigger. Nothing happened! At first, I was relieved. I hadn't wanted to steal it, let alone be responsible for keeping it. Matt and the others started laughing. He grabbed the weapon from me and pulled down on the round, wooden piece underneath the barrel, chambering another round.

"It's a pump action," he said, handing it back to me.

Embarrassed, I lifted it to my shoulder, wanting to hit something now, and fired. Glass splinters flew everywhere! Not being used to the recoil, it nearly knocked me to the ground, Matt was able to catch me in time. Laughing, he took the weapon.

"All right, my man." He chuckled. "You're going to be the keeper of the piece for us."

I was about to protest, make the excuse that Wayne was a better choice, not willing to tell them the real reason, that I was afraid Ethel might find it if I kept it. I never got the chance. A blue and white police car came cruising around the corner. Looking the other way, we saw another one coming up the street with its lights off. A few of the fellows broke and ran, heading across the park. Matt grabbed me, stopping me from following them.

"Hold on!" he warned. "Too much light that way. Down here!"

He took off running down the alley as fast as he could. Wayne and I took off after him, careful not to trip over garbage can lids and empty wine bottles that littered the foul-smelling dark alleyway.

Wayne was cussing. "Damn curfew! It ain't been long enough for them to roll on us about firing the shotgun. It's the damn 11:00 o'clock curfew I bet you! Ain't this a bunch of shit!"

Matt broke in, giving directions. "This way," he yelled. "This way; come on!"

He ducked into a pitch-black gangway at the opposite end of the alley. Stopping at the exit leading onto the street, we watched as a squad car sped past, turned at the intersection, and began searching the next block over.

We waited, taking advantage of the time to catch our breath. Everything seemed unusually peaceful during those brief moments. I sat on the concrete walk of the passageway, listening to the conversation a man and woman were having in the apartment above our heads. She was on his case about being involved with another woman. From across the street came the sounds of a radio that was turned up too loud. The mellow lyrics of The Impressions singing "Gypsy Woman" floated on the warm night air.

Matt tapped on the stock of the shotgun I'd forgotten I was carrying, breaking the spell of tranquility that'd come over me. Taking the shotgun, he put it in the leather case he still carried.

"We got to stash this thing," he was saying as he handed the weapon back to me. "Come on."

He ran across the street and onto the vacant lot next to the house with the noisy radio. Wayne and I followed. Before we could make it across the street, the patrol car swung around the corner. We ran faster.

Pulling to the curb in front of the empty lot, the cops stopped the car. Looking over my shoulder, I saw one of the officers letting a German Shepherd dog out of the back seat. I tried to tell Wayne and Matt what was happening, but they were too far ahead of me, already turning into the alley. The shotgun was slowing me down.

As I turned into the alley I decided, *To hell with this!*

Making for the nearest garage, I threw the shotgun on top and began climbing up the garbage cans on the side to get on the roof. Wayne looked back and saw what I was doing. He must have thought it was a good idea. Grabbing Matt from behind, he nearly tore his shirt off trying to stop him.

"Wait, man. Wait a minute! On the roof! Let's get on the roof!"

They climbed on top of a garage half a block ahead of me. For a brief second, there was silence, then I heard the dog barking, growling as the police turned into the alley, shining their flashlights and poking the beams into each walkway and garbage can.

When they got to the garage I was on, the dog started snarling, refusing to go on. I had to do something. Luckily, the garages were the kind that were connected together, six in a row. Not waiting for them to come up and find the shotgun, I began jumping from garage rooftop to rooftop while the cops yelled for me to stop. The dog went crazy, barking and growling. I could hear one of the cops running alongside the garages, trying to spot me with his flashlight.

Ahead of me, I could see Matt and Wayne taking advantage of the confusion I was causing. They dropped over the side of the last roof and into the street. For a split second, I panicked. If I went that way, the dog would run me down. There was only one thing to do. Running to the yard side of the garage, I dropped from the roof into the grass.

The dog acted like he had rabies, ramming into the wooden gate leading to the yard so hard he almost tore it off the hinges. Not waiting to see what would happen, I ran through the front gangway at full speed into the street. The cops and crazy dog would have to come all the way around the block because they keep the gates padlocked to the alley. They couldn't get in without a key.

Once I'd made it to the street, I knew the neighborhood and yards that didn't have dogs in them. I started looking for shortcuts through the streets that would let me travel unseen. Home was the only safe place I was able to think of. I headed in that direction, keeping to the gangways and alleys I knew so well. All the while, I could hear the sirens in the distance.

After fifteen minutes, I made it to the back door of the apartment building. Relieved, I ran up the stairs, nearly forgetting I'd snuck out earlier that evening. Slowly unlocking the door, I paused to listen. Everything appeared normal. Creeping through the kitchen past the black and white television set that was still playing in the living room, I slipped out of my clothes and got into bed. There were about five minutes left of the movie on the late show, and when it ended, I'd get back up to turn it off. My clock read eleven forty-five. I couldn't believe it! Only an hour and forty-five minutes had passed! It felt like a lifetime.

The national anthem came up on the "boob tube." I'd been laying there for nearly an hour, thinking, unable to sleep. I wondered if the police had busted Matt and Wayne or if they'd climbed up on the garage roof and found the shotgun?

Getting up and turning the TV off, I went back to bed. Finally, I forced my eyes closed. But my mind kept sending out the alarm, telling me I had to find a way out of the Chi-town ghetto and away from what was happening to me. I began to pray.

Memory Bank Activated: 3-15-1977
Subject: Egyptian Cobras
Content: 1961, Master Seven

The next morning, I practically ran to school, anxious to find out the outcome of the events that transpired the previous night. Turning into the second-floor hallway, I spotted Matt at his locker. Going over to him, my mind was primed with a million questions. His only response to my interrogation was a grin and telling me not to leave after school because we had to have a meeting.

At three-fifteen that afternoon, Wayne was waiting for us when we came out of the school building. The three of us walked toward 16th Street. As soon as we were out of earshot of any of the other kids, they began questioning me about what happened after we'd gotten separated the prior night.

"It's a good thing you left the shotgun on the roof," Wayne was telling me. "If the cops had seen you with it, you might have gotten your brains blown out."

Matt backed him up, "Yeah, they shoot first and ask questions later in this neighborhood, just like in the cowboy movies." They both laughed at the comparison. Personally, I didn't think it was funny.

In a few minutes, we'd reached the alley where the police had nearly busted us. Showing them the garage the weapon was on, I stood lookout, while Wayne, cupping his hands, gave Matt a boost up the garage and onto the roof. In a few seconds, he reappeared at the edge and dropped the shotgun over the side to Wayne. After climbing down, he took the weapon and handed it to me.

"You're the keeper of the piece, aren't you?"

He grinned his funny little grin and walked away. Wayne pulled on my shirt and handed me a large plastic bag he'd found that was reasonably clean. I used it to cover up the gun case, so you couldn't tell what it was, and stuck the stock under my armpit to hide it the best I could, hoping I would make it home without getting stopped. Wayne gave me a little push from behind.

"Come on, let's go! We got work to do."

We followed Matt as he headed back towards 16th Street. The next step was to find a place to work on the shotgun. Matt informed us that he'd already solved that problem. Taking us to the vacant tenement next to the apartment his family lived in, we silently made our way up the front stairs and into one of the first-floor units.

Like most of the lower rent districts, the West Side of Chicago was covered with buildings that had fallen into disrepair, yet parts of the structure remained sound. There were signs the place had been used before. Empty wine bottles, cigarette butts, and discarded food cans littered the floor.

Matt told us to lay low until he got the tools needed to work on the piece. In less than ten minutes, he returned with a hacksaw and a file. Fifteen minutes later, the barrel and part of the stock, up to the handle grip, lay on the floor.

Wayne wanted to test the sawed-off shotgun, but Matt said there wasn't time. We had a meeting with the Cobras in a few minutes. Besides, it was better to check it out after dark in a suitable place. Still not satisfied, Wayne kept fooling around with the piece. He began running around the empty apartment, playing like he was having a shootout with some imaginary foe. Matt and I stayed in the kitchen where we had used the rust-stained sink as a cutting table while working on the shotgun. Now that he'd brought the subject up, I again questioned him about the Egyptian Cobra initiation. He was on the verge of giving me some insight into what would take place when we heard sounds at the front door.

Matt jumped off the sink he was sitting on. "Damn!" he shouted. "I told him to wait until later to check out the damn piece!"

He ran into the vacant living room. I was thinking Wayne had gone outside with the shotgun. At first, I was hesitant, then decided I'd better follow them. I wasn't prepared for what I saw when I stepped into the living room.

A buzzing alarm went off in my head, and the warning light in my brain clicked to a brilliant white. Wayne was at the front door with his back to me, and in front of him was a towering, well-dressed Black man. At first glance, the scene looked hilarious to me. Wayne was just standing in the opened door, looking down and shaking his head like a child being scolded by a parent. Then the shotgun came into view, like a picture taken by the camera in my eye; this stranger was holding it, not Wayne.

The signals from my mind were right. Something *was* wrong. Continuing to shake his head from side to side, Wayne backed slowly away from the man. That was when I could see the pistol in his other hand pointing at Wayne's chest. He had been shaking his head back and forth, asking the man not to shoot him.

Panic hit me. What was he doing here? Was he the police? The questions ran rampant through my mind. Stepping into the room, he hooked the door with one leg, closing it behind him. He lay the shotgun down; putting a finger to his lips, he cautioned us to be quiet.

Inching across the room, he peeped into the now empty kitchen. Then, with cat-like movements, he moved over to the bedroom and peered through the slit made by the hinges on the door. Satisfied that the apartment had no other occupants, he spoke for the first time.

"Move over there with your friend, you two," he told me and Matt.

Matt had his back turned to the man with the gun. Using his eyes and hands, he threw Wayne and me a few signs, letting us know we should try for the window that was behind and to the left of us the first chance we got. That chance never came. In a voice that sounded as if he was well educated, the stranger asked us to move against the wall on the other side of the room, putting the window out of our reach as a possible escape route. We hung there, suspended in time and space.

I studied the man while we waited for a break in the silence. Something about him didn't seem to add up—his clothes, for one thing. He appeared to be much better dressed than the detectives I'd encountered. From his dress and speech, I would have said he was a big-time lawyer or businessman. Matt was the one who broke the ice.

"Who are you?" he asked.

The man hesitated briefly, then smiled. "I'm the police."

A sick feeling came to the pit of my stomach. His answer didn't appear to phase Matt, who loosened up a little.

"You ain't the police!" he sneered. "My uncle's the police, and they don't carry guns like that!"

Looking at the weapon more closely, I saw that it was silver and an automatic, not a revolver. Not able to contain it, the smile broadened on the man's face.

"You punks think you're smart, don't you?" He tried to get back into his tough-guy act, but it wasn't working.

Finding my voice, I spoke up. "Well then, if you're the police, show us your badge."

Wayne put his two cents in. "Yeah, show us your badge!"

Still playing the con, he kept on with the tough guy act. "Look, I don't have to show you punks anything! You broke into this building, plus you were turning this shotgun into an illegal weapon!"

Wayne pushed it a bit further. "And what have you done? You say you're a cop, and you ain't got no badge, the wrong type of gun. You must be…."

I finished the statement for him. "…You must be wanted for something yourself, sneaking around with a gun."

His odd behavior continued. Laughing openly, he said, "Okay, here's my badge."

Taking a wallet from the inside pocket of his suitcoat, he opened it and flashed it in front of us quickly. I expected to see a metal shield, but the only thing I was able to make out was some type of identification card with a picture of a government building printed on the facing, and he had his name covered with his fingers. Seeing that, we all started getting loud. Matt was the boldest.

"You got to come with something better than that! If you ain't got no proof you're the man, then you ain't got no reason to hold us here!"

Before he could muster a response, we heard what sounded like a herd of buffalo coming up the stairs and down the front hall. The funny feeling returned to the pit of my stomach. Maybe the man hadn't been lying. Maybe he was some kind of special police, and his colleagues were coming to his aid. When the door flew open, a flood of relief washed over me. It was Morris! And with him were a dozen of the gang members. Police or not, this stranger was in a lot of trouble now!

What happened next only served to confuse me even more. Morris and the well-dressed man greeted each other like long-lost brothers, shaking hands in that special way I'd seen only once before between the deacon at my uncle's church and the man selling the *Muhammad Speaks* newspapers.

Baffled, I turned to Matt, who for some reason hadn't seemed as puzzled as I was. Patting me on the shoulder, he turned on one of his crooked smiles and reassured me everything was cool. Morris's voice rose above the din of noise created by the group crowding into the living room, calling them to silence.

"You two, come over here." He pointed at Matt and Wayne, who crossed the room as quickly as possible. "Okay, what's happening with your friend?" He nodded in my direction.

"He's alright," Matt said offhandedly. "No problems I could see; he thinks on his feet and seems to be trustworthy."

Morris turned to the stranger. "He's the one you've been talking about, the sleeper?"

The man nodded. I began to feel like a goldfish in a bowl. Everyone in the room was looking at me, and I was completely in the dark as to what was happening.

Wayne spoke up. "He was surprisingly good last night when the cops nearly busted us. I think he's got a lot of guts."

The well-dressed man shook his head in agreement. "And he doesn't panic when things get tough; he'll need that later on. Let's give him the ritual."

"Right!" Morris said. "Thumper! You run the show!"

A muscular boy around seventeen stepped out from the crowd and stood in front of me. He tapped his chest with his thumb. "My name's Thumper! I'm the Warlord for the Mighty Egyptian Cobras! And to be a Cobra, you got to know how to handle yourself. That's what we're here to find out." He yelled, "Pee Wee!"

Another boy about my size moved into the semi-circle that'd formed in the middle of the room. For a moment, nobody moved.

Then Morris shouted, "Well, get on out there!"

It took a few seconds for it to sink in. They wanted to see us fight! I didn't know what this Pee Wee had in mind, but I had no plans of getting hurt just to join their gang. Wanting to back down, I thought of the lesser of the two evils. If I refused to go through with it, I might end up getting beat by the whole gang.

Reluctantly, I moved into the circle with Pee Wee. Lucky for me, he had the same idea of not getting hurt when it was unnecessary. We confined our punches to the body, only throwing a few punches to the head. After two or three minutes of heavy punches to the body, Thumper was satisfied and called a halt.

Then came the oath of allegiance, a ceremony conducted by candlelight. This was concluded by everyone leaving the room except the stranger and myself. With the doors closed to the kitchen and the bedroom, the only light came from the candle that had been placed in front of me as I kneeled on the uncovered wooden floor. Standing behind me, the man's voice floated on the stillness that lingered in the room.

Very slowly, he spoke.

I want you to concentrate on the flame of the candle and listen closely to what I am saying. These words are for you and you alone. Everyone has a place in time and space. Everyone has a reason, a purpose for existing. Find out your purpose in this existence, and you will know who you are, and what you are here to do, the reason for your being. You will be given a mission by this Brotherhood of Men. In order to accomplish your task, you will be given skills and training, enabling you to know the true nature of the world. You have been given a mask to hide behind. It will appear that you are a thug and a hoodlum. This is not true, yet no one must know what your true nature is. For if your inner self is revealed, there are elements in the world that will seek your destruction. There will be many who think as you do, but they are in the future. Together with them, you will form a Brotherhood of Men that will change the world. For now, you must remain the 'sleeper.'

He continued, "Your brothers will contact you at unannounced times. You must learn to trust your vibrations, the good thoughts that enter your mind. Do not think of yourself as an ordinary person, for you are not. A special path has been laid out for you to walk upon. When you return to the streets, you are to forget all that I have said and tell no one. These words are for your ears alone!"

Kneeling in front of the candle, the silence lingered for a full five minutes while my mind fought to sort out the logic of what had just happened and what he'd said. Although things were vague, a feeling of understanding arose from a far corner of my brain, telling me to be patient. Things would soon be made clear.

After the oath, the gang filed back into the room, and someone produced a couple of quarts of beer; they passed them around as the boys moved about the apartment. Night had fallen, and with my head still spinning, I drifted away from the main group and into the bedroom. Perching on the windowsill looking out at the city, I sat there, thinking. It was October, and winter was coming early. Snow was in the forecast.

Morris's voice pulled me back out of the clouds that covered the skyline.

"Screw talking, man!" He and the stranger were having a hot debate. "Give us some guns!"

The man moved out of the doorway into the bedroom. Leaning against the wall, he had a look on his face like a teacher who couldn't get through to his pupil. Morris followed him into the room, trying to make his point.

"Guns, man! That's what we need! And you tell us we got to set up some kind of propaganda machine of our own? There ain't time for that! The police are shooting us down every day, and no matter how much we talk about it, it won't get us anywhere!"

A thin smile creased the man's lips. He seemed to be in complete control of himself. With a businesslike approach, he remained calm.

"Look, Morris, I told you the plan we've decided to put into action. If you want to play madman and shoot up the place, go ahead. I'll use the Vice Lords or one of the South Side gangs."

This had a calming effect on Morris. He went over to the window, looking out at the coming storm and the lights of the city.

"I still don't see what writing and talking about what's happening to people of color is going to do to help us. We need to defend ourselves," he said in a subdued tone.

"But will you do it under the circumstances we've agreed upon?" the man in the dark suit asked him.

Morris thought for a moment, watching the storm clouds gathering. His answer came with the sudden burst of rain and hail against the naked windowpane.

"Yes, the Cobras are in; we'll do it!"

Puzzled by all that was happening, I still felt that somehow, what they were discussing concerned me in some way. Wanting to clarify the afternoon's events, I turned to the stranger, but he was gone! Without a sound, he had vanished. I started to run into the next room to see if he was there, then decided Morris might be able to answer some of my questions.

"Who is that guy that just left; what's his name?"

Morris stared at me but didn't answer.

"What is he, some kind of spy or something?" I said it half jokily, not expecting an answer. The way Morris looked at me and gave a little laugh, I could tell he caught my joke.

"Yeah, I guess you could call him that. His name is Master William Seven."

Lost in thought, he continued to watch the storm out the window. "Yeah, he is a spy in a way," he said. "A spy for the Brotherhood."

Memory Bank Activated: 3-20-1977
Subject: 1962
Content: The Bubble Gum Capers

"They've got you brainwashed, fool!"

Wayne was shocked. We hadn't expected the rebuttal that came from Morris. All Wayne had said was that President Kennedy should send the Marines into Cuba.

"Do you know who the Cubans are? Well, do you!" Morris was practically shouting, talking more to all of us than just Wayne, who tried to defend himself.

"Yeah, I know who they are. They used to be Spanish before the United States stepped in."

"Spanish and Black!" Morris corrected him. "Cuba used to be one of the slave ports used to funnel Black people into the Southern United States. Black people like your great-grandparents! You may even have some distant relatives still living there. And you want the President to send in troops with bombs to blow them all to hell? You're about an ignorant asshole!"

It had been that way most of the winter. Morris or one of the other older gang members was assigned to give us some type of special training apart from the regular activities of the "Midget Cobras," as the boys under high school age were called. Our latest lessons consisted of current affairs. We'd been hanging around the store on the corner where I lived, listening to one of the new transistor radios that'd recently hit the market. The topic on the Black radio station WVON had been the Cuban missile crisis of 1962.

After Morris's temperamental outburst, everyone became quiet, content to listen to the music the disc jockey, E. Rodney Jones, was playing and lounge on the side steps in the warm spring sun. We were waiting for three more Midget Cobras to join us. They were assigned to help us with what we nicknamed Bubble Gum Capers.

This was an assignment coming from older gang members who were no longer active in the gang; we called them "the elders." They came up with ideas and planned the missions for us.

There was a novelty and candy company that controlled most of that type of business on the West Side of Chi-town. A Black business had started an enterprise of its own. The novelty company didn't like the competition. They forced the store owners to refuse to take vending machines from the Black outfit. The Cobras vowed to change the situation.

When the three boys arrived, we joined them and headed for the store that was to be our first target. It was located about half a mile from my house on Roosevelt Road. Morris stayed outside, covering for us, while the six of us went into the store. Matt, Wayne, and I walked up to the counter facing the storekeeper. All three of us started talking at once, asking for different things. When he'd turn to get what one of us had asked for, that person would change his mind and ask for something else.

After taking him through these changes for a minute or two, he finally saw that we were putting him on. This made him angry! He began cussing, ordering us off the premises. Refusing to leave, we taunted the man, jeering at him. He became so angry that he chased us from the store. What he didn't know was that while he'd been busy with the three of us at the counter, the other three boys had silently walked out of the door with his new set of twin vending machines. This was the first of the "Bubble Gum Capers" we pulled during the summer of 1962. By the time school started that fall, we'd hit nearly every store and shop in the neighborhood.

The Bubble Gum Capers changed a lot of the gang members' ideas about hustling, and some felt it was a more productive type of ripping-off the man. Some even felt we were aiding the community, helping to foster Black businesses.

Memory Bank Activated: 3-21-1977
Subject: Knowledge of Brotherhood
Content: 1962-First Love

We were slowly dropped from the "pack," that was what we called the groups of fighters who invaded other gangs' turfs and defended our own. Packs of boys between the ages of 10 to 18 roamed the streets of Chicago after the sun had gone down. The police, unable to control the multitude of half-grown, weapon-carrying youths, always decreed it a holiday whenever the first winter snow fell upon the streets, knowing this act of nature was the only thing that kept them locked safely in their individual homes, and not on the prowl looking for a rumble.

When the rival gangs met by plan or accident, that might possibly turn thirty zip-gun, chain, and knife-carrying teenagers against the two police officers, who happened to turn a corner in their squad car and run into one of the frequent wars between the rival gangs. This could be deadly for police officers.

Some of the boys spent five or six years in the pack. I ran in the pack for four months, then Morris pulled seven of us out, saying that we'd been picked to form a special section.

With the snow and ice came a need to find places with a roof over them. Morris helped us out there as well. We were used to his leading us to stop intruders coming onto our turf or a raid into Vice Lord's territory. It was difficult to get used to the changes he introduced. Most of our time that winter was spent at places like the Better Boy's Foundation, different churches, and working out at the professional boxer Archie Moore's gym, which was not too far from my house. It became an after-school routine for Morris and some of the others to stop by and pick me up on their way to a Bible class or community rally.

Some of the guys made a few wisecracks about the Bible classes, getting especially loud one evening. We were coming from one that was conducted by a Catholic priest for the Boy's Club. They walked in the rear of the group that'd gone to the classes, laughing, and making fun of the priest and what he had said. Morris suddenly turned on them.

"Shut up! Stupid fools!" His temper was flaring again.

"The message you need was in what that old man was saying! All laws are based on religion, and laws are what they use to control you. You better shut your mouths and learn what the 'man' is using to run everything with, and that's his laws. That's the weapon he uses against you, and it comes from the ones in the Bible. He changed the way he uses them, so they work for him and against you. The first thing they tell you in court is that "ignorance of the law is no excuse. That's why they can keep you dumb and stupid and put your ass in jail, whether you knew what you did was wrong or not. Do you think the Vice Lords are your enemy? You're wrong suckers! They aren't the enemy that's hurting you. It's the man keeping us dumb and stupid, fighting among ourselves. It's time to start using our heads instead of our fists to fight!"

I looked at their faces, and they seemed to understand practically nothing of what he'd said. Personally, the feeling that all the things we were learning about related to me in some way hadn't left since the day of my initiation into the gang. The question that remained in the rearmost regions of my mind was why a bunch of hard-core ghetto street gang members spent most of their time listening to religious subjects as part of their duties to the gang.

Remembering what Master Seven's warning had cautioned me of, I kept my mouth shut and let the question slide for the time being. Morris' outburst was the signal that his tolerance was at an end. The boys started making excuses about having to be home or having to get ready for an upcoming trip over the Christmas holidays. It was easy to tell that everybody would be glad for the vacation away from Morris and the seemingly endless classes. The group split up, and I walked home alone in the freshly fallen snow.

Passing the spot where the boy had gotten hit in the eye, the incident came back to mind. Since joining the gang, I'd had little trouble with the other kids trying to muscle me; in fact, Ellis and the old gang avoided my presence like the plague. To mess with an Egyptian Cobra was pure madness! I was happy things were turning out the way they were. The difference between the old and the new activities the gang was involved in brought a smile to my lips.

"Well, you're mighty happy about something."

The statement startled me. I'd been lost in my own world and hadn't noticed the young lady coming out of the store on the corner. It was Regina, a girl around my age who went to the same school I did. We'd become friends, often meeting on the way to and from school since we lived close to each other. I'd become attracted to her warm, soft mannerisms and budding young physique. My smile broadened.

"Something must be mighty good to you," she repeated with a smile of her own. "Want to let me in on it?"

Not knowing how to begin explaining it to her, I shrugged it off. "It's nothing, just something I was thinking about."

Coming down the steps she put her hands on my shoulders. "And what have you got to do right now? There's someone I want you to meet."

Not waiting for me to answer, she took me by the arm, pulling me in the direction of her house across the street. Liking what was happening, I followed along. The mysterious person turned out to be her cousin, Gloria, who was visiting from Arkansas.

Gloria looked almost exactly like Regina, with her medium brown complexion and long curly hair. Both of them were a couple of inches taller than me. She laughed at the introduction, making a comment about how short and cute I was.

Noticing that Regina's parents weren't at home, I asked about them. It seemed strange the way they whispered and giggled when I asked the question. Laughing, they came over to the couch I was sitting on and sandwiched me in between them. Regina had a funny gleam in her eyes, while the hint of a smile played on her lips. Gloria started playing with my ear with one hand and rubbing my inner thigh with the other. Regina cuddled closer, whispering in my ear.

"Billy, have you. ever made love to a girl?"

I wasn't ready for the question. Their closeness and the touch of their hands stimulated me; what were they trying to do?

To say no would be too embarrassing. Fighting to calm down, I forced the lie out.

"Sure, why?" I said with as much confidence as I could muster. Gloria planted slow, lingering kisses on my neck and around my ear.

"Good," Regina said. "Because I want you to make love to Gloria."

I didn't understand. From everything I'd heard about sex, the man was the one who did the asking, not the woman, and certainly not for someone else.

"It's not that I don't like you," Regina told me. It's just that it's that time of the month for me. I can't do anything, but Gloria can. Since it's Christmas, I thought you wouldn't mind giving her a present." They both laughed.

I sat there, not knowing what to say or do, or if they were teasing me or not. For the better part of a year, I'd get this unusual feeling in my genital regions whenever encountering a girl I liked. Regina and Gloria had awakened that feeling. The only problem was that I had no idea what to do with my raising nature.

Gloria broke in, "I bet he's never done anything. He's probably still a virgin."

Insulted, I retorted. "Only girls are virgins!" I regretted the words as soon as I'd said them, realizing how stupid they must have sounded.

Regina laughed. "That's okay! Gloria will show you what to do."

Dazed, I tried to resuscitate the mobility that'd left my limbs. I was unable to move. Gloria pulled, while Regina pushed me into a small room in the back of the house.

Shoving me through the door, Regina, giggling, closed it like she was afraid I'd try to slip out before the door fastened, shutting Gloria and me in the tiny guest room.

Walking over to me, this girl I'd met only a few minutes earlier put her arms around me, kissing me full on the lips. Pressed tightly together, we stood there in the middle of the room. I felt myself getting more excited each time she ran her hands up and down my back. Finally, the embrace was broken.

Leaving me, she went to the edge of the bed and immediately began taking off her clothes. Stripping down to thin laced panties, she lay across the bed and motioned for me to join her. Climbing into the twin-size bunk, she stopped me.

"No! Take your clothes off first!" she said with a smile.

Turning around, I stripped down to the boxer shorts I was wearing. When I turned back around, she was laying on the bed naked.

"How old are you?" I asked, not knowing why the question came to mind.

"I'm fourteen. Why?"

I'd never seen a nude girl before.

"Oh! Nothing, I just was wondering is all."

She dismissed it with a shrug of her shoulders, beckoning with her finger.

"Now," she said. "Come here."

I eased myself on top of her. At first, we lay there kissing and grinding against one another.

Then she said, "You got to put it in."

I didn't know what she meant. Seeing that I was lost, she chuckled and took hold of me with her hand, sending hot flashes through my genitalia. Slowly, she guided me inside her.

It was a new and wonderful experience. The feeling of her soft, smooth body moving under me was intoxicating. I'd just begun to enjoy this new stimulus when suddenly, she started moaning and thrashing her hips wildly from side to side. Confused, I didn't know what to do. Maybe she was having some kind of epilepsy attack. Maybe she was dying or something! I made a move to get up.

"No!" she said, out of breath. Grabbing me tightly around the waist, she pulled me back into her. "Don't stop now." She told me. "Just a little while longer."

She seemed to be in pain and enjoying it all at the same time. The logic of this eluded me. She began to move even more profusely, the moans becoming sharper. All at once, her body tensed, and she collapsed under me. We lay there across the bed, listening to our breathing and the sounds that filtered in from the streets. I didn't want to stop; my body was telling me I needed to finish. There was a wet sticky substance between my legs, and I thought maybe she'd been injured by her frantic lovemaking; but at the same time, I felt like I needed to add my own sticky stuff to hers.

Before I could move, Regina came busting in the door with a wild look on her face. "Quick! You've got to get out of here!" she was saying. "My parents just drove up in front of the house!"

I jumped up, not caring if Regina saw me or not. Pulling my pants on, I sat on the bed to put on my shoes.

"No time for that!" Regina hissed.

Grabbing the rest of my clothes, Gloria and Regina pushed me down the hall into the kitchen. Stuffing the shirt, jacket, and shoes into my hands, Regina opened the back door and pushed me out into the yard, slamming the door.

Standing there half-dressed, I stopped to put on the rest of my clothes. I was tying up my shoelaces when Gloria came out of the house. Maneuvering me around to the side of the building, she kissed me for the last time.

"You know, you're okay for a virgin man."

Grabbing me, she squeezed lightly, chuckled, and ran back inside the house. I went home to take a bath and contemplate the new stimulus called sex that had entered my life.

Memory Bank Activated: 3-24-1977
Subject: Disbandment Midget Cobras
Content: Out on My Own

At the age of fourteen, I ended up on my own. The incident that caused me to leave came with the spring weather of 1963, less than a couple of months before graduation from grammar school. It was during the city of Chicago's "clean-up" week, or vacation, as the school-aged kids called it.

Mayor Richard Daly's picture and voice took on the fictitious air of being everywhere, telling the city residents to clean up the dirty streets. At the same time, the schools were closed for spring vacation. Hence, the name "clean-up week vacation." Ethel had gotten off Aid to Dependent Children and was working at one of the large laundry and dry-cleaning companies on the near West Side. Leaving around seven o'clock each morning, she'd rarely forget to remind me about taking care of my younger brother, Reotha, whose carefree five-year-old existence came under my supervision during that week's vacation.

Getting up a little after nine o'clock, I fixed breakfast for Reotha and myself, then straightened up my room.

Morris dropped by about ten o'clock, telling me the gang was having a meeting at Franklin Park and it was mandatory for me to be there.

Ethel had given me strict instructions not to stray too far from the apartment, a tall order for a young teenager on a warm spring day. Taking "Re" (my brother's nickname) a couple of houses down the street to the Robinsons, I asked the oldest girl, who normally watched him for Ethel, if she'd keep an eye on him for a couple of hours.

When I made it to the park, it was too late. The meeting had already broken up. Morris, Matt, and Wayne were the only ones left. Matt told me what the meeting had been about. The gang was breaking up; at least the Midget Cobras part was.

At first, I refused to believe it! My oldest brother, Leroy, had gone down to St. Louis to live with our father at the beginning of the school year. His chances of finishing high school without having to join the gang were better there. Joe couldn't afford to take the three of us, so Leroy was chosen.

Now, with the gang breaking up, I would be alone in the streets. We'd been each other's protection and companionship for a number of years. Besides, I'd grown fond of many of these young "hoodlums of the mind." The breakup was due to many things. Graduation was only a few weeks away, and most of us would be leaving Mason grade school and going to different high schools in the city. Also, Matt's parents had decided to move to Decatur, Illinois.

Morris saw the news was getting me down. He suggested we go to the lecture that was being held at the Boy's Club, saying I might be interested in what they had to say. The lecture turned out to be more of a sermon, similar to the other functions Morris made sure none of us missed attending. After a while, the "pie in the sky" type of religious sermons I'd been hearing about God, the devil, and good vs. evil, had become clear to me. I could see the different entities working in everyday life. Everything discussed was about the here and now at these gatherings. Each time I came away with a clearer understanding of how religious beliefs among people played their part in the world I was living in.

Leaving the meeting, I could see the impact everywhere, religion governs the laws, morals, and even the eating habits of the humans we passed on the streets; yet few people seemed to be aware of it. The city blocks were crowded with winos, junkies, conmen, pimps, and whores, lost people who saw no hope for a better life. My mind's eye took it all in like a 16 mm movie camera.

I was checking the footage in the projection room of my brain when I opened the door to the apartment. Ethel was all over me before the door closed behind me, calling me lazy and no good. I didn't understand. Then Re came out of the living room.

So! I thought. That was the problem. She was mad because I'd left Reotha with the Robinson girl.

She continued on her rampage.

"I told you to look after your brother," she yelled, "but you don't do anything I tell you! And what's so bad is you left him locked outside all day without anything to eat!"

"But I did feed him this morning, and he was supposed to have lunch at the Robinsons." I tried to explain. "Look!"

I pointed to the plates and dirty silverware in the sink. She refused to believe me. "You probably fixed something for yourself!"

I looked at Re in desperation. I sensed that he was unable to understand what was happening or was unsure if he'd eaten or not. Ethel stormed into her bedroom, returning with a belt.

"Wait a minute," I said, feeling that I was being falsely accused and had gotten too old to be getting a spanking like a little child.

"I'm not going to let you whip me for nothing!" This got her even more upset.

"What you going to do boy… Are you gonna fight me?"

"No!" I said. "But I'm not going to stay here and let you whip me for something I haven't done. I'm getting too old for that anyway!" I opened the door.

"Billy, don't you go out that door!" she yelled.

When she was that way, I knew it was no use talking to her. I stepped out the door and started down the stairs. Ethel came to the top of the stairway.

"If you go out that door, she screamed, don't ever come back in this house. You hear me, boy?" By that time, I was walking out the downstairs door, closing it softly behind me.

Fading sunlight flashed between the brownstone brick buildings. My mind whirled as the shock of what had just happened sunk in. I was on my own with no place to stay!

My brain was racing in high gear; to me, it was logical that every fourteen-year-old kid stayed with his or her parents. So, where were my parents? One had just told me to get out of her house and don't come back. The other was hundreds of miles away and had said he couldn't afford to take me in. I was truly on my own.

It wasn't only because of Re not getting his breakfast, which was untrue. I could still hear one of Ethel's favorite expressions she'd say to family members and friends.

"That boy thinks he's grown, walking around like he's forty years old! Don't do anything I tell him to do. Always talking about going to a meeting or something; don't do anything but run the streets with those hoodlums! I should send him to his father. That's what I should do!"

My father!

Thinking about what she'd said so frequently gave me the answer to my problem! I could go to St. Louis and live with Leroy and Joe; he'd have to take me in since I was homeless. The thought was calming, taking me back into a state of serenity.

Then I realized I'd been running down the street. That was why the sunlight seemed to be flashing between the buildings as if I were in a moving car. Slowing down to a walk, I put my mind to working out the transfer from Chicago to St. Louis. Another message flashed in my brain. School, what about school?

Graduation was three weeks away. From the hard knocks the Chi-town streets handed me, I knew one of the things meaning the most to me later in life would be the knowledge of what was the truth about my place in this world and a good education. I'd have to find a way of staying in Chi-town until school was out in June.

Turning onto 16th Street, I picked up speed again. The warm spring sun hit me full in the face. I relaxed, running smoothly, dodging little girls playing jump rope and hopscotch along the narrow sidewalks. Besides, the gang was still together until school was out. One of them certainly knew where I could find a bunk, at least for a night or two, at least until I could straighten things out.

Heading for Matt's house, I nearly ran past them in my haste. They were two blocks from Matt's in front of the liquor store hassling a wino that had held out on the money the gang gave him to buy beer for the party that night. It didn't take them long to convince the half-drunk man to give the "little boys," as he called them, their money back.

As we walked over to Matt's building, I told him about my dilemma, asking if he knew of a place I could stay for a while.

"Yeah," he said, without a hint of emotion or having to think it over. "I know where you can stay until we get out of school."

Once again, a hopeless situation ended up with a simple solution. What I needed was provided, as if by some miracle or pre-planned chain of events. Matt, Wayne, and I somehow ended up living in his folks' apartment without any adult supervision for a period of five weeks. His father had to leave in order to meet a deadline to be on the new job waiting for him in Decatur.

The apartment became Cobra headquarters while we waited for school to turn out, and into the summer. At the same time, we were getting another, slightly different kind of education from Morris, who produced an endless stream of masters of one craft or another, all the time being versed in who we were and what we were being trained for. He really pushed hard on how this society related to us individually and as a group. Morris continually stressed the need for what we were doing to remain a secret, concealed from general knowledge. We would have to be careful at the schools we were going to and in conversation with friends and family that were not part of the Brotherhood.

Only later, after understanding more of the world, was I able to relate to the full impact of what had been taught to the small group of Black youths by the elders living, for the most part, in our own community.

Memory Bank Activated: 3-26-1977
Subject: Graduation
Content: Spreading of the Seeds

Up until the day we graduated, most of our time was spent in the apartment or some other location in a learning situation. I made out with the bi-monthly checks Ethel received from my father for child support. She'd been surprised when, three days later, I dropped by and gave her my new address and telephone number. She agreed that she would cash the checks and hand the money over to me. My independence was a sore spot in our mother/son relationship that summer, but slowly softened. Resigned to the fact that I was not returning, she gave in to my independent ways. That was the beginning of the friendship that existed between us.

Graduation from grade school came with a mixture of joy and fear. We were all happy to be going to high school finally. It's the dream of every student in junior high. For me, the fear came with the idea of the gang breaking up. Nobody liked to talk about it. All of a sudden, it was time to take the class picture and walk down the aisle.

Gathering at the apartment that warm June morning, we listened to Morris's speech telling us that we were "seeds" from one tree, and by spreading out we would become like a forest, sinking roots wherever the seeds landed, and yet still be a part of the parent tree.

Acting as if the class picture was an event of great importance, he had insisted that Matt put in an order for a copy for him because it was a thing to remember. A majority of the gang members are captured in that photograph.

Memory Bank Activated: 3-28-1977
Subject: 1963 - St. Louis, Missouri
Content: "Sleeper" by the River

Jazz flowed out of the heavy wooden combination of hi-fi and radio. My sensory awareness picked up the fact that it was the same piece of furniture I'd grown up with in the early 50s, only now it held a rich, deep, glossy shine from the numerous waxing of the dark cabinet over the years. Taking the trumpet out of the case, I began cleaning and oiling the valves. Joe Ware was one of the quiet people. For this I was glad. He rarely asked about my activities in Chicago and placed no restrictions on my movements. We'd gotten along fairly well, considering we were strangers to each other, having met only once or twice a year for brief periods in the eight years following our exodus with Ethel to Shaw, Mississippi.

Lying on the bed, I did an imitation of the broken-hearted trumpet player, trying to look like Louis Armstrong using the cleaning rag like his famous handkerchief. I'd been in the school band for a short period back in grammar school, and Joe had picked up a used trumpet from the pawnshop for me to practice with. He loved jazz and had an extensive album collection.

As I lay there wishing I'd stuck with the music lessons, what Morris said at the last meeting flooded my mind. "You must assimilate into your new lifestyles and blend with the people around you. Do as they do, only be careful that you don't pick up their bad habits, like getting drunk on cheap wine and wasting your time shooting craps for nickels and dimes on the school playgrounds. Remember, stay cool, don't let the day-to-day grief you're going to get from people hassle you. If you blow your air of tranquility, you'll lose this game we're playing. It's just like sleeping, he'd said. "Take what you've learned and go to sleep with it. One day, a Brother's going to tap you on the shoulder and ask you to wake up. Until then, just sleep on it...and wait."

So I was waiting.

The early 1960s, we'd been told, was the beginning of the "Age of Aquarius." We'd also been told by the Brotherhood that by the mid-70s that the vast majority of common people would awaken to the true nature of the "Beast" that misused many for the benefit of a chosen few. I wondered what this transformation would look like. This awaking of the masses was still a decade away

Since coming to St. Louis, I'd once again felt like a fish out of water. The kids there lived by different rules and communicated on a different wavelength than I was used to. Even in Chicago, it had been difficult to socialize with people who weren't members of the gang. At the new school in St. Louis, I stayed mostly to myself.

Joe wanted me to attend the same school Leroy graduated from, Hadley Technical. Unbeknown to him, Hadley was to be merged with another regular high school that year. At the start of the term, the two schools joined under the name of the latter, Vashon. Taking Morris' suggestion, I settled down to living a more normal life.

Most of my time was spent in the company of my brothers-in-law; a couple of guys around my age called June Bug and Mickey, brothers of his wife Hannah. When not with them, Joe would find some activity for me to get involved in, going to the Cardinals baseball games (he got tickets from his job at the Modern Jacket Co.), or time was spent simply rapping to me about jazz and the great performances he'd seen. Sometimes he and his girlfriend traveled hundreds of miles to catch a performance. Jazz could be heard continually coming from the red brick duplex he rented from a woman whom we all called Aunt Bee. She was a soft-spoken lady who lived with her mother, a woman of full Indian descent. Each time I went with my father to pay the rent, she'd insist that I stay long enough for her to read a chapter or two from the Bible. The lady held a fascination for me, inspiring me to learn as much as I could about the real Native Americans, not the Hollywood version. I learned how the country was stolen from them. After a period of time, I looked forward to the visits and listened to her as she sat in her wheelchair, stricken with age, unable to move. The only reminiscence of her proud past and heritage was carried in her long, black hair that she kept in two large braids. Thinking about her and the verses she read brought to mind what we'd learned in the Brotherhood classes with Morris.

Thoughts of Chicago made me homesick. Then it hit me as I lay on the bed; this place (St. Louis) was my home, not Chicago! Laughing, I took the mouthpiece out of the trumpet and put the instrument in its case.

I didn't know what my eventual mission would be, but the need to keep myself together was something I couldn't shake. The night before graduation I'd asked Morris for his address so I'd be able to keep in touch.

"Don't worry," he told me, "we'll get in touch with you." Before I could push it any further, he'd slipped out of the apartment.

I left "Chi-town" the day after Matt's father came back to finish clearing their stuff out of the apartment and pick him up. I declined an invitation by Matt and his folks to spend the summer with them. They had treated me like a member of their family. Only, I thought looking in the other room at Joe Ware doing paperwork and paying bills, I have my own family. Laying across the bed, I drifted off to sleep, thinking about the Cobras and wondering what the people here would say if they knew I was a "sleeper," resting momentarily by the big Mississippi River.

Memory Bank Activated: 3-30-1977
Subject: The Winter of 1963
Content: Return to the "Windy City"

The peacefulness of the St. Louis environment lasted less than a year. Before the end of 1963, I was once again living in Chicago. This time on the South Side at 8341 Rhodes Street with Uncle John and Aunt Dot. The incident that caused my leaving St. Louis happened during the week following the assassination of President John F. Kennedy.

Used to a faster lifestyle, I'd come up with a scheme for generating a few extra bucks, besides the five dollars a week allowance I received each Friday. Noticing that the young men in the neighborhood liked to spend their time shooting craps in empty hallways and alleys, I convinced them to use the summer cottage behind our house as a kind of club headquarters. After putting in some tables, a friend I'd met at school nicknamed "Popeye" and I would run card games and act as the houseman for the popular dice game that took place each afternoon. We also set up a small roulette table I'd found among the stuff stored in the backroom of the cottage. The setup ran smoothly for a while, increasing my income, sometimes by thirty to forty dollars a week.

Joe was unaware of the hustle I was running. I made sure that the games were over before he arrived home from work. Then one day I returned to the house to find him waiting for me. He was plenty mad about what I was using the cottage for, or rather what he'd been told was happening. It seems that after the game that day, some of the boys returned to the cottage without my knowledge with a young girl. One of the neighbors across the alley watched them feeding her wine and then taking her into the summerhouse.

"There were four or five of them," she told him. "And the girl was so drunk she could hardly stand up. It wasn't hard," she said, "to figure out what they had in mind. And gambling went on nearly every afternoon!" She thought Joe should know what kind of son he was raising.

Even though I knew nothing about the incident, I was still to blame. Joe and I agreed it might be better if I were to stay with my Aunt Dot back in Chicago for a while. So, here I was, back in Chi-town, but on the South Side, sitting in the apartment watching a documentary of Martin Luther King's "I Have a Dream" Speech on television. The amount of media coverage the event had gotten earlier that year let me know that what this powerful speaking Black man was saying was of great importance. Uncle John sat in the large reclining chair watching the tube with an intense look on his face, while Aunt Dot and Johnnie Bee, her cousin, sat at the dining room table. They disagreed about a passage from the Bible and its meaning. Often, they taught me from it and when things got hot, I would find myself left out of the conversation.

After seeing them together, it didn't take long for me to figure out they were as close as if they had come out of the same womb together. But this time, I was glad they'd blocked me out. I had a lot on my mind. Watching the massive crowds of people on the television screen, my mind drifted back to what happened a few hours earlier.

I was on my way home from the donut shop I worked at part-time. When school started, Aunt Dot insisted that I give up working there full time and concentrate on my classes. I'd gotten on the bus heading south, when all of a sudden, a man literally fell into the seat next to me, pinning me in. At first, I thought he might be some kind of freak trying to muscle me. I was going to elbow the man off when I noticed the bloodstains on his clothes. This caused me to take a good look at him. It was Morris!

I sat there, unable to speak. Putting his finger to his lips, he motioned for me to be quiet. Dazed, I sat there, looking at him. His clothes were torn and dirty, and his face was puffy, like he'd been in a messy fight. When the bus reached 63rd and Cottage Grove, we got off. I could tell he was hurt pretty badly.

Turning down a side street I had to help him because he couldn't keep his footing. Taking him into the first hallway we came across, I propped him up on the steps of the building. After that, I didn't know what to do. We hadn't seen each other for over a year and here he pops up out of the clear blue sky.

What is this all about anyway? I let the question linger in my mind, not asking out loud.

Sensing my curiosity, Morris asked me. "Bet you're wondering what happened, and how I knew where you were."

He wanted to laugh, but the pain from his wound stopped him. I asked the question anyway. "What happened…how did you get like this?"

He told me about a rally that a group he'd helped organize had given earlier in support of the civil rights movement. They started a march on the West Side headed toward the suburbs. Things had just gotten underway as the head of the procession passed the last L-stop before Cicero when a train pulled into the station, and out poured a gang of white youths carrying sticks, chains, and anything they could get their hands on. They tore into the crowd of Blacks, who were mostly older people and kids, attacking and beating them.

As Morris talked, emotion overcame him, and he forgot his condition. He cussed the police and the city officials, saying it was a frame-up. The attackers even knew the names of the organizers of the protest march, making them their primary targets. The police who were observing hadn't interfered until warrants for the arrest of the leaders of the march arrived.

I tried to calm him down. What I really wanted to know was why he came to me, and how did he know where I was? The one time I'd gone back to the old neighborhood, I'd been told that everybody in the gang was either dead, in jail, or moved away, and I hadn't given my address to anyone over there on the West Side.

So I asked him. "Say, how did you find me?"

"Find you?" He laughed, which caused him to clench his teeth.

"We never lost you, little brother."

He kept laughing until the pain made him stop. Then he became serious.

"I need your help, brother. I'm going to have to play dead for a while. Until I find out if this is part of a campaign to wipe us out or just a bunch of freaky accidents. I want you to do me a favor."

He gave me an address of a friend of his about ten blocks away from our location.

"We kind of work together," he said, "so they may be watching his place. I can't take any chances; I have to know for sure. You got to check it out for me."

Not knowing what else to do, I agreed. Moving him around to the back of the building, I left him tucked in a dark corner under the back porch. Going to get his friend, I prayed he wouldn't die in the dark cold alley.

Forty minutes later, his friend and I returned in his station wagon. Loading Morris into the back, I got ready to jump into the front seat when he stopped me.

"Where do you think you're going?"

I hadn't thought, acting more from reflex. I just assumed that I would be going with them. It'd always been that way with the members of the Cobras. Morris disagreed.

"The best thing you can do for me is take your butt home."

His friend started the motor. I stood there with the door open. Morris raised up on his elbows and looked at me.

"When it comes your time, you'll know what to do. Just don't let them push you into making a foolish play or jumping the gun. Stay cool and stay out of trouble. Thanks for your help, little brother. I knew I could count on you."

He leaned over and pulled the door closed, and they drove off.

Listening to Rev. King, the words of the man came with more meaning than before. Looking at him on television and hearing his philosophies of non-violence, I began to wonder if the violent world we lived in would let this man of peace continue his work. It became clear that I would have to become more knowledgeable about myself and the society that surrounded me in order to survive, especially if I followed the non-violent pattern this man was setting.

Memory Bank Activated: 3-31-1977
Subject: Milwaukee, Wisconsin
Content: Move to "Brew City"

The apartment on 83rd and Rhodes was usually quiet, with both Uncle John and Aunt Dot working. This gave me lots of time by myself. They rarely pried into my past or current activities. It wasn't hard to see that my well-being and not control was their main concern. It showed in everything they did. But fate has in store an ever-moving life for the Aquarian.

Once again, I suddenly packed up and moved to another location. This time, it was a judgment call of my own, the decision coming after a weekend visit to Milwaukee, Wisconsin. My sister Delores was living there, and during the Christmas break, I'd gone up to the "Brew City" to spend a couple of days with her. She lived on 12th Street in an upper flat rented from a slightly senile Black preacher, who was a mason by trade. I'd talked to her about a week earlier, and she'd told me that her ex-husband, Thomas Manning, was in town. That was the reason for my visit. After their separation, Delores stayed with us while waiting to move to Milwaukee. Manning, watching the house, had tried to break in to get at her after we had all left and she was alone. It was behavior like this that was the reason she'd moved to Wisconsin.

It'd been the same during most of the three years they were married. He and I tangled before I'd left Chicago for St. Louis over his fixation on torturing people. When he tried to muscle me a short time after meeting him, I had ridden the L trains from the South Side, where he and Delores lived, back to the West Side, returning with the sawed-off shotgun. Delores begged me not to kill him, more for my sake than his. I shouldn't have listened to her.

Now, he was in Milwaukee, and so was I. After being there one night, I made up my mind to move from Chicago. At sixteen, school seemed boring when it came to the regular classroom curriculum. At least, that was the reason I gave Aunt Dot for quitting school to make the move to Milwaukee. She didn't believe me and couldn't understand why. My grades were good, above average in most subjects. I believe she would have tried to physically stop me from leaving if I hadn't told her the real reason for the move.

I loved my sister and didn't want anything to happen to her. Manning was a madman, and I believed him capable of even murder. She cried but agreed. The next weekend, I moved into the apartment with Delores and her daughter, Angel.

Memory Bank Activated: 4-2-1977
Subject: Milwaukee, Wisconsin
Content: 1965- U.S. ARMY

Milwaukee has a small-town atmosphere and is set in the heart of a major northern industrial metropolis. Everyone comes looking for the fast hustle and bustle of New York or Chicago. Milwaukee isn't like that, and it may throw you at first. After a couple of weeks, things seemed to have slowed to a crawl for me. There was extraordinarily little of the paranoia found in the streets of most major cities. The people, instead of avoiding contact or communication, actually spoke and greeted each other when meeting in the streets like in a small rural town.

It took a lot of getting used to. Delores was working as a typist at the Army Reserve base, while Angel stayed with an elderly lady two houses away, during the day. The weather was starting to clear up, so I took to the streets.

At first, I was more or less shown where the happenings were by my cousins; Aunt Rosie's husband had moved from Chicago a few years earlier to pastor a local church in Milwaukee. After a short period, I began moving around on my own, usually walking, and checking out the people and the neighborhoods.

Knowing Manning, he would have some kind of contact close to where Delores lived. He was probably already aware that I was in town. The only thing to do was hang loose and wait for a sign of his presence. The sign I got wasn't the one I was looking for. It came from the Brotherhood.

My Milwaukee contact was a young Black ex-paratrooper by the name of Michael. I'd spotted him casing me and got the little warning vibrations in my head. For a week he'd pass by me a few times each day, as I sat on the front steps, catching the sunlight in the afternoons. At first, I thought he was just someone living in the neighborhood. Then he began to materialize at other places I'd happen to be. I could feel him observing me. Not knowing who he was, I let it slide, but kept an eye on him.

One Friday, after a week and a half of checking me out, he made his move. Instead of walking past as he did daily, he stopped and asked me for a match, and I said I didn't have any. He acted like he found some in his pocket. Lighting his cigarette, he paused to look at a girl that walked past.

"Milwaukee got some fine-looking women, huh? Not like the West Side of Chicago."

The little hair bristled on the nape of my neck and the alarm buzzed inside my skull.

"You from Chicago?" I asked, putting on a smile to relax him and at the same time position my body so I could move with greater ease in case of danger.

"No, I'm not from Chicago," he said. "But I used to spend a lot of time there, got a Brother over there by the name of Morris."

Then I relaxed; he was one of us. We sat on the steps, and he filled me in on what my next phase of training would be. He was to prepare me for military service. At first, I couldn't believe my ears. How was I supposed to join the armed forces when I was only sixteen years old? He told me not to worry; it was done every day. He'd teach me everything I would need to know. What the Brotherhood wanted me to do was lead as normal a life as possible, forget about everything else, and keep under wraps what I'd learned under their tutorage. Michael had a message from the elders.

"Remember, you carry the message. That's orders from Master Seven and the elders. So forget about Manning."

I exploded; telling him that was something I couldn't and wouldn't do. To hell with what they said I was being trained for. I had no idea what all the reading, studying, and information they fed me was good for anyway. My family was threatened, and I'd be damned if I just walked away and forgot it.

Michael saw my point. Calming me down, he said he would check into it and see what could be done about the problem. but I wasn't to take any action on my own. They didn't want me to get into any kind of trouble.

The next day, Michael stopped by the house. He had found out where Manning was staying while he was in Milwaukee. When night fell, we walked the three blocks over to North Avenue, then west to 15th Street. Before turning onto the one-way street, Michael stopped me.

"Look, they told me to tell you, you're only to talk to him. We don't want you to get hurt or end up in the pen for killing him, okay?" I agreed.

As we were leaving, the very thing I didn't want to happen happened. Turning the corner, we ran into four young men. One of them was Manning. We stood there looking at each other. I could tell he was surprised to see me.

Michael knew one of the men. They greeted each other slapping five and shaking hands. Manning broke the silence between us.

"Huh…Billy…! I'd heard you were in town. How long are you going to be here?"

It was a leading question, and I wanted to be led. I smiled,

"Permanently. I'm staying with Delores."

I wanted to make sure he got my meaning. He acted like he was only making small talk.

"And how is she doing? I haven't seen her for a while."

Remembering how he had treated her in Chicago, I wished I had a gun so I could pop a couple of slugs in his ass.

"She's fine," I told him, "and getting better all the time."

They were on their way to one of the small bars on Teutonia Avenue. Michael put on a front like it was Saturday night and he was ready to party, talking loudly and messing with the ladies that passed by. At the tavern, Manning was up to his old tricks, trying to get me drunk on sloe gin. I stayed away from the gin and drank a beer, surprised the bartender didn't ask me for some ID.

I tried to pump him for a little info on what he was up to here in Milwaukee, but he wouldn't take the bait. After that, I made an excuse about having a date and left. Michael stayed with them, talking it up and drinking with them, trying to find out what they were up to. I hoped he would have something to tell me later.

Bound to the Brotherhood, I had to keep my oath, but I also had to keep the oath that is handed down to all male children: the protection of family and loved ones. Both of these things were dear to me.

Memory Bank Activated: 4-4-1977
Subject: Military Induction
Content: Boot Camp–1965

My presence seemed to have some effect on Manning's behavior. He got really friendly, and after about a month, he even wormed his way into visitation rights, coming to see his daughter, Angel, periodically. My job was to make sure I was around whenever he was in the house. Three months later, Ethel moved over from Chicago into an apartment on Third Street.

Delores was still believing that some miracle would happen, and everything would straighten itself out. Knowing Manning, I tried to make her see that something like that just wasn't going to happen. She kept hanging on, not saying so, but hoping for her little girl's sake. Personally, I was hoping the situation would change before it was time for me to leave. Michael told me it would take a month for him to brief me and teach me the physical side of what I needed to know about military life. He was a little hesitant at first, saying I had no business getting this type of training, coming from the new "Love Section" of the Brotherhood as I did.

Most of the young brothers they sent to him were athletes or natural street fighters. I was short, thin, and didn't even look the sixteen years I claimed to be. The others who'd gone the route at least looked old enough to join the army; for the entire time we were together, he kept repeating that fact.

Meanwhile, he got me a job working with him at Northland Carwash out on Good Hope & Teutonia Avenue. That fall, the work at the carwash picked up and so did my training. It was the perfect place. Michael and I could talk without any problem, and it was easy to slip away for a few minutes. One of Michael's cousins worked on the crew with us. The majority of the time, his house became the first stop for everybody after work. It was there that I to meet the Brothers who were in the Milwaukee branch of the Brotherhood.

During the few weeks I was under Mike's supervision, three instructors were assigned to the carwash. One worked with us for two weeks. It was interesting to see a middle-aged man with a master's degree trying to "bust suds" washing cars and conducting a one-student class at the same time.

After four weeks and one day, Mike decided it was time to start the paperwork to get me inducted into the service.

Ethel hit the roof when I told her I was joining the army. She refused to sign the papers and wanted to know where I'd gotten a birth certificate that said I was a year older and could join the military with a guardian's consent. I thought the best cover was to say I'd done it myself. I didn't want my mother to interfere because I was still a minor.

After two days of useless procrastination, I went to Mike, thinking he could come up with some solution that'd get her to sign. What we decided to do was have the Brotherhood section chief talk to Ethel. The cover we gave him was as an army counselor. He looked the part in his Brooks Brothers suit. His job was to show her how beneficial it would be for me to join the service. His rap sounded like the same type of line an army recruiter will hand you. He dropped by the house the next day, and with both of us pressuring her, she signed the papers. On November 29, 1965, I became a member of the United States Armed Forces.

After the induction, my first assignment was USA REC. STA. ET. Leonard Wood, Missouri. I arrived on the 30th of November, 1965. The army was nothing like I'd been told; it was worse.

The pressure started with a loudmouthed drill instructor coming on the bus and yelling his lungs out. It was 3:14 in the morning. The tactics had the effect he wanted. Most of the half-asleep young men were mentally traumatized by the sudden use of verbal force. We were in for one hell of a brainwashing, one that lasted the entire time I spent in the military.

After three days of being harassed and bombarded with military ideology, they thought we were programmed and scared enough not to desert, so they assigned us to the C Company 3rd Battalion -3rd Basic Combat Training Brigade., then let us go to the post PX for a couple of hours. Sitting at one of the tables, a couple of the other recruits and I were drinking the three-point-four beer the army allows them to sell on the base.

The conversation was getting dull, and I still couldn't figure out what I was doing there. Becoming a soldier had nothing to do with the prior training and education I had received. Not being able to figure it out, I left the table and went over to the side of the building that housed the penny arcade. Walking over to the row of pinball machines, I dropped a coin in the nearest one. Getting into the game, I didn't pay much attention to the trainee who got the machine next to me. I'd gotten a pretty high score with extra balls when he spoke to me.

"You play a nice game."

The voice sent an instant recall into my brain. Turning, I looked and there was Morris!

This was unimaginable. The last time we'd met was a year earlier in Chicago when he'd been wounded.

"What are you doing here?" I asked the question a lot louder than I should have, not able to contain myself.

"Never mind," he said, "just keep playing the silver balls, and listen to what I'm going to tell you." "You probably can't figure out why you're here. We have our reasons for placing you in an environment like this. This will be part of your training and a test for you. So far, your training has dealt with the humanitarian side of the Brotherhood. With the world in the state it's in now, it's necessary for you to become aware of what exists on the other side of the coin. Here you will learn what war, hate, and destruction can do to a human being. We'll guide you and set up the contacts, but your survival will depend on you, and you alone. Master Seven sends his best wishes and hopes that you will have a safe journey through the "valley of death."

"Don't forget who you are, and don't forget the Brotherhood. Remember the message you carry." Then he walked out the door.

The contact with Morris helped me to withstand the remaining weeks of basic training. The short leave they gave us at the end of bootcamp felt like it was heaven-sent. The only sour note about the graduation from boot camp was the rumors, rumors we believed were circulated by our trainers, saying that most of us in the class would be given advanced infantry training (AIT), then shipped to a little-known war in a place called Vietnam. I had signed up for airborne (paratrooper) training. The rumors became believable to me when I received orders to proceed to Fort Gordon, Georgia, for infantry training immediately after my leave was up.

Memory Bank Activated: 4-5-1977
Subject: Advance Infantry Training - Airborne Training
Content: The Mean Green Psych Machine - 1965-66

My leave lasted from the twenty-ninth of January, 1966, until the thirteenth of February. I had to report one day before my birthday, Valentine's Day, the only day this country dedicates to the ideology of love. The orders read Co. C - Seventh TNG-BN - Third TNG. REGT. US ATC, Fort Gordon, Georgia. This was a training company specializing in preparing men for paratrooper school and Vietnam. There was little talk about becoming a paratrooper and a lot about the war in Vietnam. Many of the men, including myself, knew little or nothing about the war in Vietnam.

There were maybe fifteen seconds of news coverage given to the conflict on the nightly television news in early 1966. We all wondered why most of our time was spent learning guerilla warfare tactics and not skills an airborne trooper would use. After eight weeks of camping out in the

Georgia woods, they felt we were tough enough to go into combat and jump out of an airplane without breaking every bone in our bodies.

On the fifteenth of April, I arrived at the fourth STU.BN TSB - Fort Benning, Georgia. I thought the drill instructors in boot camp and A.I.T. had been rough. The Airborne NCOs were maniacs! A normal day ran like this, and I mean ran! At 3:00 A.M., the sergeant comes into the barracks and clicks on the lights, then chews everybody out because we weren't standing at attention before the light came on. From 3:00 A.M. until eleven or twelve o'clock at night, they kept us on the go. You couldn't walk in the company area. If you were in the company area, only running was permitted. If you were caught walking, it cost you twenty push-ups. While the fine "art" of throwing yourself from a plane moving at 130 to 160 miles an hour was taught to you, they kept putting on mental pressure.

One game they liked to play went something like this: First, the sergeant would call the trooper to attention. Then, standing nearly on a trooper's toes, he would shout in his face. "Soldier, would you make love to my wife?"

The soldier is surprised, not believing the question. "Huh, sir?"

The sergeant shouts in his face: "DON'T CALL ME SIR! I WORK FOR A LIVING! I said, would you make love to my wife, you stupid ass cherry!"

The soldier, getting nervous, answers, "No, Sergeant!"

The sergeant replies, "What! She isn't good enough for you? Drop and give me twenty push-ups!"

The soldier drops to the ground and does twenty push-ups, then jumps back up standing at attention.

Sergeant: "Okay, let's try it again. Would you make love to my wife?"

The soldier answers, "Yes Sergeant!"

Sergeant: "What! Why you good-for-nothing home-wrecking cum freak! You mean you'd wreck my marriage? Drop and give me forty more push-ups!"

This type of thing would go on all day and into the night. After two weeks, we had passed the "Ground and Tower" training, which was a hell of a lot of P.T., learning the PLF. (parachute landing fall), and jumping from 35ft and 250ft towers while strapped to a harness, hooked to a line, running from the tower to the ground.

The third week was to be spent qualifying. It took five jumps to get your paratrooper wings, or as the veteran troopers called it, "busting your cherry."

I had a problem. In order to stay connected with me, the Brotherhood had gotten word to me that I would have to be assigned to one of the units with the 101st Airborne Division.

Finishing jump school with the class I was in would ship me out two weeks earlier than needed, according to the unit replacement schedule. This class of troopers would end up going as replacements for airborne units of the 1st Cavalry Division.

The solution came with my first jump. We were waiting on the runway of the airfield for the Air National Guard that did the flying for the trainees at Ft. Benning. There were a few minutes before boarding, and everybody was talking, trying to keep the shakes away. The conversation got around to the morbid subject of how many different things had happened to some of the less fortunate "riders of the silk." It was then that I got the notion, *What if I was injured on this jump? Why not?* It was a common thing. The trick was substantiating a short-term injury and nothing serious.

When they loaded us on the Cl30 aircraft, I was the second man on. This meant I'd be next to the last coming out of the plane. Jump doors on the Cl30 are closer to the tail section. A few minutes from the drop zone, the jumpmaster stood us up. Each man had to go through the procedure of checking the chute of the man in front of him. We turned around and went through the same checklist, thereby checking each other twice. Then the signal came to "hook up," letting everybody know it was time to fasten the ripcord from our chutes to the long, thin wire that ran above the rows of seats that lined the walls of the aircraft.

After "hook up," the next command was "stand in the door!" The two lines of troopers (one on each side of the plane) did what they called "The Airborne Shuffle" to the two open doors at the tail end of the plane. This is a special way of moving with full jump gear and rifle pack aboard a flying aircraft. Turning and facing into the open doors, the first troopers to reach the doors slapped their hands against the outside edges of the door in preparation to exit. You could feel the tension as everybody watched the small red and green lights mounted on the door next to the jumpmaster's face. The lights flashed from red to green.

The sergeant dropped the arm he had been holding above his head and yelled, "Go!"

The line started "shuffling" down the space between the two rows of seats. Then suddenly, I was there, standing at the door.

The jumpmaster pointed at me and yelled, "Go!"

I heard the command, yet it seemed unreal. My reflexes snapped me into a jump stance, locking elbows into my sides, I lowered my chin and jumped into the prop blast from the propeller of the C130. It slapped me back and down under the tail of the aircraft. I fell, tumbling, seeing sky then ground, then sky again.

Then I remembered the "count to four" that I was supposed to do. The experience of the first jump caused me to forget the slow count after leaving the plane. I started counting, one thousand, two thousand, it was too late; the force of the chute opening came as a shock. I thought I'd hit the ground.

Looking up, there it was! The most beautiful thing imaginable to me was the large piece of green silk with cords hanging from it. I wanted to climb on top of it and kiss it!

The jump had been normal, except my risers were twisted. Spinning my body in the opposite direction, I straightened them out. We'd jumped at the low altitude of three hundred and fifty feet, which was the combat height for quick insertion. It takes very little time to reach treetop level from that height.

After checking out the chute and equipment, I had less than thirty seconds before "treetop-level." It was only half a minute, yet it gave me a feeling of total freedom. Made me want to fly like an eagle, fly across the country, fly to the sea. I transcended with the elements, and for a brief few seconds, was in harmony with the universe.

Taking hold of myself, I looked around. The trees were coming up fast. Checking my memory bank, I forced myself into the "PLF. position," put my feet together and bent my knees. I grabbed the parachute's raiser cords, tuck my chin down, and pulled the risers into my chest. The wind blew me slowly toward the plowed-up field that was used as a drop zone. Finding myself coming in on an angle I tried to turn my body to the front. The best PLF is made from the front. Too late, I smashed into the ground! Someone or something must have been looking out for me. My body automatically reacted, flipping me over in a PLF

A sharp pain shot across my body. For a second, I sat there on the ground, too elated to move. I'd jumped out of an airplane! The pain had stopped, so there was nothing seriously wrong, just the force of the landing, I thought. It felt like it had been more than the thirty-five mile an hour we had been told was about the fastest rate of descent. Glad to be alive, I laughed out loud and sprang to my feet. Suddenly, a message of intense pain jammed the receivers in my brain. I fell back to the ground. It was my left ankle.

Trying to move it brought more excruciating pain. I could feel it beginning to swell. Leaning back on my hands, I burst out laughing.

Things like this had been happening to me all my life. The very thing I needed had been provided for me. With a badly swollen ankle, I couldn't possibly finish qualifying for another couple of weeks, just enough time to make the quota that was coming up for the 101st Division. Sitting there laughing, I pulled in the parachute and stuffed it back into the pack. A sergeant drove up in a jeep.

"What the hell's wrong with you, boy?"

His heavy Southern accent and racist tone sounded comical to me.

"Nothing, Sergeant" I got back on my feet.

He shouted something about getting my chute over to the pick-up truck, before it drove off. One of the troopers saw I was injured and stopped to help me.

"What's so funny?" he wanted to know.

Still laughing, He helped me limp toward the equipment pickup truck.

"This will probably keep you from graduating next week," he told me.

"You're right. It might," I said. The smile stayed on my face for the rest of the night.

Memory Bank Activated: 4-8-1977
Subject: The 'Nam 1966
Content: Valley of the Shadow of Death

We traveled the coast of Vietnam capturing or killing the Viet Cong. No matter where Charlie runs, no matter where he hides, he just can't get away from old eagle eyes.

—Vietnam Campaign Fight Song of the 502 Inf. 101st ABN Division, Summer 1966

My orders read HHC 2BN ABN 502 Infantry USARPAC - APOSF 96347.

They put us in summer dress uniforms, then took us to the airport. We looked like a bunch of young soldiers going on leave. No one seemed to notice or care that many of the young men would die before the one-year tour of duty was up.

The stewardess on the plane gave us the businessman special, including movies, drinks, and lots of smiles. On the twenty-second of June 1966, at 3:47 A.M. Asian time, I stepped off the luxury Boeing 707 onto Vietnam soil.

The heat and stink hit me in the face and took my breath away. I smelled death in the air. A soldier in green jungle fatigues came running up to the loading steps of the plane. It was night and pitch-black, making it impossible to see anything.

He was shouting, "Move your butts off the airfield and into the terminal. This plane has to be out of here in less than ten minutes!"

Everybody was moving as quickly as possible into the one-story building. The heat and humidity were unbelievable. It must have been close to ninety degrees at four o'clock in the morning. The soldier who met the plane filled us in on a few things, that we would be taken in squads to Camp Alfa which was a few miles from the Saigon airport, and during the ride under no circumstances should we uncover the closed flaps on the truck.

"You are in a combat zone," he said. Make no mistake about it. If you don't do what you are told, it may cost you your life. Remember that, and welcome to the 'Nam."

Yeah, I thought, *welcome to the valley of death.* I asked myself, *Why am I here?*

***

I'd seen Michael on my last visit to Milwaukee. He'd been a peacetime soldier, and he didn't have any info about actual combat or Vietnam. Wishing me well, he'd left on another assignment.

Everything seemed to be okay with Delores, or so she said. When she told me she didn't want me to leave, I thought it was because of the danger I would be in and dismissed it as sisterly love, not seeing it was something different, something she wasn't telling me. Bidding her and Ethel goodbye, I stopped in Chicago to see Aunt Dot and the rest of the family. Then on to St. Louis to talk with Joe Ware. He and Ethel still couldn't figure out why I called them by their first names. It was not out of disrespect for them, just my particular kind of love for my parents.

After making the excuse that they wanted me at the deportation station in Oakland, California, I'd left a week early. The real reason was I wanted to see as much of California as possible before shipping out. There was a good chance I might not make it back to the States at all.

***

Bouncing along in the back of the truck, I thought about the people back in the States. They didn't even know what was happening out here. Vietnam was only thirty seconds' worth of news that flashed across their television screens each evening. Pulling into the Alfa compound, we unloaded and were placed in quarters for the night.

The next morning, I woke up to the music of the Mamas and the Papas singing the song "Monday, Monday." It played over the compound loudspeaker forty or fifty times that day.

At first, I couldn't understand why the song was so popular. It was an old tune back in the States. Then a trooper told me what the lyrics meant to the men who were coming into the country and going into combat.

"Monday morning gave me no warning of what was to be, or that Monday evening you would still be here with me."

Then he explained it to me, "Look here, blood, on the orders they just gave you, you going to the 101st Division, right?"

"Yeah," I answered, not understanding.

"Well, if you join your company this morning, you might not be alive this afternoon. They've been seeing a lot of action, with heavy casualties."

This became more obvious when they called the replacements for the 101st to headquarters and gave us travel orders to our units. We'd been told that we would be at Camp Alfa for a week. I was there less than twenty-four hours.

A "Caribou" aircraft took us to Phan Rhan, home base for the "Screaming Eagles" of the 101st Airborne Division. The battalion was out on operations in the "boonies," as the troops called it. When we came in, they said indoctrination and climatizing would take seven days. We were there in the rear area for two days, then they sent me out to my unit in the field. I was assigned to headquarters company 2/502 Inf. battalion.

In the States, I'd been trained on a 106mm Recoilless rifle as a specialist, anti-tank indirect fire crewman, tank killers, they called us. Since neither "Charlie" (as the Viet Cong was called) nor the Americans had much use of tanks because of the jungle terrain, there wasn't much use for anti-tank crewmen.

They handed me a "black beret," an M-79 grenade launcher, and a 45 caliber semi-automatic pistol, then informed me my job was (LRRP) or "long-range reconnaissance patrol." They called me a "Recondo." They woke me up early the next morning and told me to gear up. I was going out online.

Memory Bank Activated: 4-11-1977
Subject: 1966 - The 'Nam
Content: Black Berets

The clouds cast a light grayness along the horizon. The wind was high, causing the helicopter to dip, then rev up, climbing for altitude. I could see the town of Dak-To down in the valley, a sleepy little town not far from the demilitarized zone. The "chopper" dipped once more, only this time, it kept dropping. Looking out the empty door, I could see the supply and mess tents sitting on the side of the mountain overlooking the small town. "Hootches," the name that G.I.'s gave to their one-man tents, stretched out in neat uniform rows.

The young white door gunner looked at my black beret and started shaking his head with a frown on his face. "That's one hell of a job you got there, wearing that black beret," he volunteered. "No way you could get me to do the stuff you guys do!"

The warrant officer flying the Huey went into his "hover," getting ready to land in the clearing that had been made a few hundred yards behind the main tents. The chopper eased to the ground, sending up swirls of dust from the frequently used landing zone. The pilot turned, yelling for us to get out. It was then that I noticed he was Black. It became increasingly clear that the closer I came to the combat zone, the "darker" the ranks got. Three of the six replacements coming in with me were Black.

A Spec. 4 met us on the edge of the landing zone. Taking us to the supply tent, we drew some jungle gear, then he showed us where to store our stuff until the six o'clock (eighteen hundred-hours) formation. The individual platoons we'd been assigned to were out in the boonies. It was time for noon chow, so we walked over to the mess tent.

The Spec 4 named Travis was a slim build brother in his early twenties. As we walked through the chow line, he began to fill me in on what was happening with the Recondos, and the 502nd.

Everybody at the Camp Alfa Replacement Depot had heard about the latest major operation the 101st had been involved in. I had heard about it on the plane while we were enroute to 'Nam. The news of what actually happened over here was kept from the fresh replacements and general public, but like always, the "scuttlebutt" (military slang for rumors or gossip) got around. There had been little they could do to keep it quiet about the now-famous request that a lieutenant named Carpenter had made, a request that Napalm bombs be dropped on his own position that was being overrun by the Viet Cong.

Napalm has the effect of acting like a "running fire," and they used the deadly chemical to cover a large area. Carpenter had literally called in the Napalm on top of himself and his men.

The meaning of the prayer I'd had to analyze a few years earlier ran through my mind. "Yea, though I walk through the valley of the shadow of death, I shall fear no evil." Could I really fear no evil?

During the summer of 1966, Vietnam was most assuredly the valley where the shadow of death continually moved. It was the sixth month, in the year of sixty-six. The significance of numerology did not escape me.

I thought about my father, Joe Ware, and the time he had spent in the service during World War II. During that time, the shadow of death had moved across the entire world. The thought still filled my mind, keeping me awake as we sought refuge in Travis's hooch from the intense heat of the Southeast Asiatic sun.

Travis, lying on the inflatable rubber mattress, yawned, waking me out of my daydreaming. The heat was suffocating. The humidity was as high as the temperature. It was the end of the monsoon season, and even with an overcast sky, the temperature was 100 degrees. Once in a while, a puff of cool air came down the mountain, but not often enough to make a difference. Leaning back against the sandbag wall of the hooch, I closed my eyes.

Travis raised up on his elbows. "Oh, by the way, welcome to the 'Nam!" We both laughed, knowing what he really meant was, *Welcome to hell!*

Waking up just in time for five o'clock chow, Travis and I walked back to the mess tent. While standing in line, I heard what sounded like a thousand giant eggbeaters. A swarm of helicopters appeared on the horizon. Landing two at a time, troopers poured from them, heading to the company areas to store their gear, and racing to see who would be first in line for the hot meal, which could become a luxury after a week in the jungle. Immediately I could see the comradery among the troopers, talking, joking, arguing, and fighting, giving them an outlet for pent-up anxieties. Most were just glad to be alive at the end of an operation.

After the six o'clock formation, I was assigned to the 3rd Squad of the reconnaissance platoon, which was attached to headquarters company. Then I was told, since I was the fresh new cherry, to get ready for night sentry duty out on the perimeter of the camp.

A Huey chopper picked us up from the landing zone. After a ten-minute ride, we were dropped on a small, heavily vegetated hill on the other side of town. It was my first experience in the jungle at night. We set up an *L*-shape ambush on the trail that ran thru the thick vegetation. Taking turns along with the other seven men on the night patrol, we each spent two hours on guard, slept for four, then it was two hours of guard duty again.

While on guard, it was impossible to see my hand before my face. The jungle night was pitch-black. There were no streetlights or neon signs to light up the thick undergrowth, that seemed to be alive with sound and movement. Even without being able to see, you could hear the living things in the jungle. Strange exotic insects blended their voices with animals of the jungle creating a unique symphony of sounds. The only problem was not knowing if the crawling, creeping sound I was hearing belonged to some lizard or a Viet Cong.

My mind began playing tricks on me. Tightening my grip on the M-79, I released the lever that breaks it down like a double-barrel shotgun. Pulling the 40 mm grenade cartridge out, I put a shotgun canister round in. It was filled with extra-large double odd-buck shots. The grenade round wasn't any good at close range; it had to travel fourteen feet before it armed itself. If the things going "bump" in the night weren't just my imagination, they could be on me before I realized it. I needed something that worked close range.

Nothing happened on my first watch. The second two hours ended with the sun peeping through the hilltops. Watching it coming up out of the east, I heard the sounds of heavy shells exploding in the distance. Suddenly, it came to me, there hadn't been a quiet moment since I'd gotten here. Vietnam was the noisiest place on earth. There were planes flying, bombs dropping, and gunfire twenty-four hours round the clock.

The next day, the battalion packed everything on two-and-a-half-ton trucks, and we moved out of Dak-To. A squad of men had to be placed on each truck during the convoy in order to provide adequate firepower for the caravan. Most of the hazards for long columns of vehicles driving down the two-lane highways of South Vietnam came in the form of ambush from the Viet Cong. When the column stopped, we automatically started watching the surrounding terrain.

After several hours of endless rice fields and frequent stops for water buffaloes that refused to move off the road, we pulled into a small village. The trucks had just ground to a halt when we were fired on. Everybody froze, hiding behind the sandbags piled up around the bed of the trucks. The first sergeant came running back to our truck.

"Pass the word: concentrate your fire on the farmhouse!" He pointed to a mud hut that was on the other side of a rice patty at the edge of the village. The sergeant shouted, "You with the 79, lop a round into the house!"

It took a second to grasp that he was talking to me. Putting the weapon on my shoulder and raising the sights on the barrel, I judged the distance from the road to the center of the building. Looking through the sights, I pulled the trigger.

Plop! the grenade leaving the launcher sounded like a champagne cork popping out of the bottle, but the impact of it was a different story. The shell landed on the front of the house, pelting the walls with shrapnel, tearing a large hole in it, and shaking dried palm tree leaves from the roof. The troops started pouring small arms fire into the house.

I was dropping another shell into the chamber of the M-79 when a cease-fire was called. Without bothering to confirm the kill, the caravan moved on. Then it hit me with what I had just done. I'd possibly helped kill someone.

That evening, just before dark, we arrived at the rendezvous with the 327th battalion and other units of the

101st. Passing through the city, I read the sign put up by the engineering corps. Welcome to Tuy Hoa, Vietnam, population 25,000, a vacation spot of the Orient. Coming out of this base camp, the 2/502 would rack up one of the highest "kill" ratios in Vietnam during the fall of 1966.

Memory Bank Activated: 4-11-1977
Subject: The 'Nam–1966
Content: "Widow Makers"

"Say, Ware, wake up, man!"

It was Murphy, the ranking SP/4 in the third squad. I opened my eyes and looked at his sunburned face. He handed a small package to me.

"This is your share of the business cards we ordered."

Like many things purchased from the locals, it was wrapped in the yellow and red colors of the South Vietnamese government.

"What is this?" I asked him, still half-asleep.

"I already told you what it is!"

He shrugged his shoulders and walked down the row of Hootches, passing out the packages of cards. Murphy was a heavy-set white kid from upper Wisconsin: deer hunting country. Being from the same state made us "homeboys." Since he'd hunted deer with his father, they'd given him a 30-6 rifle with a scope and made him the 3rd squad's sniper.

A blue-eyed sandy-haired, always happy nineteen-year-old named Davis, who was from St. Louis, also called me his homeboy because I'd been born in his hometown. The third squad was the most integrated with nine men, four white and five Black.

Unwrapping the brightly colored packet, I looked at the cards. They read in Vietnamese:

DAY LA KET-QUA-CUA VIETCONGNH UNG

NGUOI DA TAO CHO VO HO THANH QUA PHU

In English, they read, "Compliments of the strike force Widow Makers." In the bottom left-hand corner were crossed M-16 rifles. On the right was a skull head with a parachute, the sign of death. The top corners were occupied by the Screaming Eagles patch and 2/502-strike force emblem.

"Business cards," Davis had called them. I hadn't become accustomed to the business he talked about. To him, the cards were a kind of joke. They wanted us to throw them on the dead bodies of the Viet Cong we killed as a warning to their living comrades.

We'd just returned from a "business" call out in the "boonies." Two weeks of chasing and being chased by the North Vietnamese troops and large bands of Viet Cong. Other units would tease us about the price you had to pay to wear the black beret.

A lot of the short-term missions had us working hand in hand with the Green Berets Special Forces that trained and ran operations with the Montagnard, who were allies of ours. They were skilled trackers, plus had knowledge of the I Corps region, which was the 101st area of operations along the northern coastline and highlands of South Vietnam.

Putting the cards in a waterproof plastic pouch, I stored them inside my rut sack. Everybody was packing up their gear. The entire battalion was going out into the boonies. It was my seventh mission in the three months we'd been on the beach at Tuy Hoa.

Idle for a couple of weeks, most of the troops had a short period of rest while the battalion was on "Stand-Down." There was lots of free time to swim in the South China sea or check out the "strip" that housed an endless row of different bars. Everybody had a good time except the long-range reconnaissance platoon.

Our new battalion commander, whom we called "Gunslinger" because of his white-handled revolvers, had seen fit to lend us to Special Forces for a couple of weeks. They had us catching Caribous and Huey helicopters from the D.M.Z. down to the Mekong Delta. Anytime a unit was in trouble, they would send us in, and with Green Berets working in two and three-man teams, they stayed in trouble.

So while the rest of the 101st took a holiday, we saw enough action for me to get a combat infantryman's badge and get acquainted with the men in the third squad.

After those couple of weeks, all the units ended up going into action. They were calling it, Operation "John Paul Jones."

Memory Bank Activated: 4-13-1977
Subject: The 'Nam–1966
Content: Operation John Paul Jones

The favorite tactic of command was to send out the recon outfits a few days before bringing in the rest of the combat companies. Operation John Paul Jones started out as usual. Coming in low under the pre-dawn light, the formation of helicopter gunships hovered over the small clearing. Guys started complaining about the six feet drop to the ground. It was like jumping without a chute with the sixty to seventy pounds of equipment everybody was carrying. As usual, it didn't get us anywhere.

The pilot said, "In five seconds, I'm taking the chopper back upstairs."

There was a line of Huey's waiting to unload the rest of the platoon on the landing zone. They rarely kept their aircraft at a low altitude, it increased the chance of getting shot down. Helicopter crews lived with a high mortality rate.

Dropping to the ground, Sarge moved us over to the side of the landing zone, forming a ten-man squad. Davis was on the radio. There was a lot of chatter coming in. I wondered why they built us up to ten men. Usually, there were eight of us. All the squads had been beefed up that way.

Crouching down among the bamboo, the rut sack dug into my shoulders. This was the hardest part of a patrol. With a full pack of rations and ammunition, we would hump the boonies in the heat, insects, leeches, and sudden death.

After the other choppers dropped the remainder of the platoon, each squad was assigned a direction of the compass and given an area within a given radius to cover. Splitting up, the four squads headed in different directions. Now I knew why we'd been given extra men; we would need the added firepower.

We moved inland from the rocky seacoast, using the gunfire from naval ships offshore to drown out the sound the choppers made landing troopers on the LZ. In less than three hundred yards down the hill, we hit elephant grass. This was better for me. I was small, five feet six inches tall. The elephant grass grew to a height of five feet, eight inches to six feet tall. A man that was taller than that would have problems. He could easily catch a bullet in the head. It hadn't taken long for me to learn the tricks of the trade.

There was a little verse I thought up about my age. *My eighteenth birthday was coming up and here I was in the jungles of Vietnam. Eighteen with a bullet, got my finger on the trigger. I'm gonna pull it.*

Viet Cong infiltrators would leave leaflets on the trails. "Chicago gangsters go home. Your fight is on the streets of America, not Vietnam. Passing some of them, I knew what their presence meant: North Vietnamese troops. They were the ones with the propaganda machines. Tension wanted to creep into my body. Taking control, I relaxed.

"Yea, though I walk through the valley of the shadows of death."

Reciting in my head, I used the verses of different poems, religious texts, and writings I'd studied to calm myself. The only way to survive was by concentrating on what I was doing.

Carrying the M-79 positioned me number two man in the squad. My job was walking behind a white boy we called Red because of his red hair. He was the point man, a loudmouth hillbilly from Tennessee. That was what he called himself, and so did everybody else. He was loud and had the bad habits of getting drunk on Colt forty-five rotgut liquor the Vietnamese sold Americans and calling brothers he didn't know nigger. Walking behind him, I thought how lucky he was it was me and not someone else covering his back. A few of the "bloods" expressed the desire to put a clip of rounds from an M-16 in his head. He'd kept me from getting killed more than once. I didn't like his mouth, but the closeness of men in combat goes beyond racism and everything else. We had a strange kind of bond. Every time he called me a nigger, I called him a jive-ass, redneck, poor white trash honky. Then I would tap the barrel of my M-79 and flash a toothpaste smile, letting him know I was the man he depended on to back him up when the shit hit the fan.

The elephant grass slowly turned into bamboo, then jungle vines. Traveling from sunup to sundown, we moved inland deep into the tunnels created by the overhead canopy of jungle vegetation while maintaining contact with the other squads via radio.

Jungle warfare creates a different fighter than other types of combat. The guerilla fighter learns to move along the narrow trails for weeks, cross streams, sit-up ambushes, and cook his meals while making as little noise as possible and never talking above a whisper.

The first day, we made no contact, so that night we ate a cold meal, and set up an L-shaped ambush with Claymore mines. Night in the jungle can freak you out, you never get used to it.

Closer to daybreak, the area was lit up with the exploding Claymore mines. Travis and Hooper, two of the Black troopers had the guard duty. With their M-16s, they sprayed the bend in the trail where the ambush was set up. Everybody came out of their nods, clicked the safety off their pieces, and peered into the darkness. It was a little after sunrise, yet we were still unable to see because of the vegetation growing overhead. The lieutenant came to the position the new man Clinton, Red, and I were manning and told us to get ready to move out. Hooper and Travis had wasted a monkey.

That second morning, the terrain started getting hilly, making the going tough and dangerous. It was a territory V.C. liked to use for large company-size ambushes. We started hearing jet fighters making air strikes a little before noon. All at once, I noticed that the natural sounds of the jungle had stopped, giving me that funny feeling you get during the quiet before a big storm. Off in the distance came a sound like thunder. From experience, I knew better. It was the jet fighters on an airstrike, and it wasn't far away. I looked back at Sarge, the third man online behind me; he nodded in recognition that the increasing sounds meant there was a battle taking place up ahead.

Using hand signals, he told Davis to make a quiet call and let the lieutenant and the other squads know about possible enemy contact, then signaled for the machine gunner Washington to move to the front, and the rest of the squad to stay alert. Davis got "Chatter" on the radio, and after talking for a few seconds, he said the lieutenant wanted us to hold our position and wait for further orders. Sarge told us to break for chow but no fires; "It may be the last meal you'll get for a while," he whispered.

Memory Bank Activated: 4-14-1977
Subject: The Nam – 1966
Content: Operation John Paul Jones

My feet pounded into the ground. It was difficult running with the pack on my back. The call from the first squad had come at the end of the noon meal. They'd hit V. C. in at least a reinforced squad strength. I listened to the machine gunfire in the distance. AK-47's made a dull thumping sound compared to the crisp, sharp one and a half-second burst of the American M-16s. It was a noisy fight they were in.

Sweat poured from under the beret and streamed down my face, soaking my olive drab jungle fatigues. Sarge gave the signal to stop. Red heard it and dropped to the left side of the trail. I dropped to the right, covering the opposite side. The squad followed our lead. After a couple of minutes, the lieutenant showed up and passed the word up to us on the point to keep our eyes open. They'd encountered hostile forces in three of the four sections we had been sent out to recon. The rest of the battalion was being called in.

Red was chewing on some tobacco. A thin line of it trickled down the side of his mouth, mingling with the stubble of red beard.

He whispered to me, "Christ! It'll take them bastards, the whole day to get out here!"

We'd been left in this situation before. Supposedly, the normal time for a company to be airlifted out to us was two and a half to five hours. The average time, in actuality, was five to twelve hours. This is a great deal of time when you were thirty-five men pinned down by two or three hundred heavily armed enemy troops. Now I knew why the gunner on the helicopter had said he was glad he didn't have the job of long-range reconnaissance.

Looking up the trail, I wondered how many V.C. waited for us a few hundred yards away.

The lieutenant told Sarge to move us out. Red got back on point, picking up the pace. He broke trail, while watching the bushes and trees, keeping an eye out for the notorious Pungi stick booby traps so we wouldn't step on them. Made of bamboo, the V.C. planted them in the ground and covered them with vegetation. They were razor sharp and could slice through the rubberized soles of the green-topped jungle boots we wore.

We'd been on the path a half-hour when the sound of small arms fire made us slow to a crawl. We could hear the men of the first squad, their sergeant directing fire. The V.C., "Charlie," was laying down heavy fire. I could hear the sounds made by their heavy machine guns, AK-47s, and mortars. The lieutenant was on the radio. He called a halt, and Sarge formed us into an assault line, then clued us in on what the situation was.

Seems the first squad had come to a stream about fifty yards up ahead. When attempting to cross, they'd been fired on. Enemy strength was indicated as possibly a light squad, maybe six men with a heavy machine gun, that had been reinforced by at least two more. What was even more important was the fact they were North Vietnamese Regulars, believed to be the 45th Infantry, which meant they knew their job.

The first squad had one dead and two wounded. Our line moved in. The strategy was to pin them against the stream with their backs to the water and the first squad. Taking the safety off the M-79, I took out the shotgun canister and replaced it with a grenade. Seconds seemed to drag by as I picked my way through the vines and undergrowth. Then without warning, the small tree to the right of my head exploded, sending a shower of wood splinters into my face. Instinctively, I dove into a prone position. Everybody was firing into the bushes.

Laying on my stomach, I tried to wipe some of the dirt off my hands in order to feel the damage to my face. Still, without being able to tell, I decided it couldn't be too bad. There was little blood, and I was still conscious, even though I was in a lot of pain. Sarge was trying to tell me something, but I was unable to hear him above the noise. Then it dawned on me to use the launcher I was carrying. That's what he wanted me to do. Looking for a tattle-tale hint of where the machinegun nest was, I spotted it as the gunner let loose with a short burst.

Leveling the sights of the 79, I fired a round into the bushes. The trees around it exploded. White smoke filtered between the overhanging vegetation. Washington continued to paste the area with the M-60 machine gun. I could see the first squad grenadiers' grenades exploding a few yards away from mine. I fired another round that looked like it was right on target. The firing stopped coming from the heavily camouflaged machine gun.

The lieutenant called a cease-fire. Smoke from the rounds we'd fired still clung to the bushes. The first squad reported that at least three of the V.C. had been seen moving down the bank of the stream. They gave chase but had lost them.

Still in the combat line, we moved toward the stream. The lieutenant wanted us to join up with the first squad as soon as possible. Passing the spot where my shell landed, we found only torn-up vegetation and some blood droppings. For some reason, I was glad there had been no bodies to count. Coming to the stream, we stood on one side, with the first squad on the other.

Since they had wounded, the lieutenant decided to make the command post on the other side of the stream. The injured men would have to be taken out by medevac. Setting up a defensive perimeter on the other side of the mountain stream, we waited for the second and fourth squads to reach our coordinates. It also gave me a chance to see a medic, who told me the only damage would be small scars on my nose and the right side of my face from the wood splinters. Cleaning the small multiple wounds, he put some kind of salve on them and gave me some for future use. Kidding, he made a joke about my not worrying, because whenever he treated a wound in the field, he turned in a report at the end of the mission. That meant I'd be in line for a purple heart. But he never made it to the end of the mission. The next day he went out on a medivac, wounded. I heard later when we got back to base camp that he'd been shipped out to a hospital in Japan. Without his medical report, there was no record of it being a combat injury.

Memory Bank Activated: 4-15-1977
Subject: The Nam–1966
Content: Operation John Paul Jones

Daybreak brought a swarm of men and equipment, and "Gun Slinger" brought in the battalion. Since we were at the location, cutting the landing zone for the helicopters naturally fell to us.

After the areas had been cleared, we were ordered to move out, this time with full platoon strength. The third squad had the point, and it didn't take long for us to run into trouble. We'd hardly started on the trail when we drew fire. There was no way of telling the size of the force we'd run into.

At first, the shots were scattered, pinning the platoon down on the path. Ten minutes later, the firing stopped. Everybody was wondering what was happening. On his own, Red decided to take a look. Sarge was in conference with the lieutenant and didn't see him crawl into the bushes. Laying there on the side of the trail, I could hear Red moving through the grass.

Sarge came up to me. "Where's Red?" he asked.

"He's out there." I pointed. "He said something about checking out Charlie's position."

Sarge clenched his teeth, looking like he wanted to hit something. "Damn him." His whisper was so low I could barely hear it.

"Okay, let's go get him. We're pulling back to the company command post."

He moved into the grass, following the trail of bent blades of grass left by Red. I fell in behind him. We kept low for about nine or ten yards, when the world turned into a Roman candle. Small arms fire and rifle-propelled grenades came in from everywhere. I could see Red a few yards ahead of us. I started to call to him but thought better of it. A khaki-clad North Vietnamese got up and ran in front of him. Red dropped him with a short burst from his M-16.

Crawling to the ditch where the man had fallen, Red raised his head above the short grass to look in. I saw the hand with the automatic pistol popped up a couple of feet in front of his face. The gun went off, blowing a hole in the side of his head. He fell face down on the ground, blood and fluid flowing out of his head. Instantly, Sarge was in a kneeling position. He fired a full clip into the neck and chest of the North Vietnamese officer that fired the pistol.

Running over to Red, I turned him over. To my surprise, he was still alive. The only thing he said was, "No, don't...."

I knew he was dying. Sarge threw me his first aid kit. Taking out the package of morphine, I jabbed the needle into his arm just under his rolled-up shirt sleeve. He became delirious, mumbling to himself. Looking at his wound, I knew the morphine was a waste of time. With the right side of his head a bloody pulp, it was a miracle he was still alive. Kneeling over him, I wanted to comfort him, but found nothing to say. He started having spasms and twitches. After about ten seconds, they stopped, and he was gone.

An eternity seemed to exist in the couple of minutes it had taken for things to happen. Repeated sounds of gunfire in the distance brought me back around. The fighting had picked up and moved ahead of our position. Sarge came out of the ditch. He'd searched the dead officer, found a map, and collected his pistol for a war souvenir.

He looked at Red. "Come on, let's get him back to the medic."

"Too late," I said. "He's dead."

Sarge cussed, "Stupid fool, why in the hell did you bring your ass out here in the first place!"

Seeing the fruitlessness of chewing out a dead man, he calmed down.

"All right, we still got to take him back for grave registration."

Both of us grabbed an arm, dragging the body as we ran the yardage back to the trail. Charlie started pouring it on after that, keeping us pinned down for the rest of the day. It was nearly dark before a medivac picked up Red's body along with the other dead and wounded. Later, we learned that we had run into a company of North Vietnamese Regulars, estimated strength around two hundred and fifty men. The firefight lasted for two days.

At the end of the second day, we had a visitor. General Willard Pearson from 101st headquarters. It seems that the 101st achieved the dubious honor of having the highest "body count" of any unit in the Nam during that time. The general gave us a pep talk and had his picture taken with us. The general was the only one in the picture with clean fatigues.

After the picture, we returned to the jungle trails. Taking prisoners, we found out we'd run into the advanced elements of the 45th Battalion, and they were reinforced by units of the 95th Infantry, crack North Vietnamese troops. Our battalion commander, "Gunslinger," decided to change his tactics. He flew in on a chopper just to talk to the "recon" platoon.

With his easy manner, he told us how proud he was of the outfit and especially us. Since we were the best he had, we could understand why he was leaving us out in the boonies on a "stay-behind" mission. This was the typical con game.

His strategy was to take the battalion back to Tuy Hoa and have them standby, ready to re-deploy within a couple of hours, leaving us to recon and report on any enemy activity in the area after our troops pulled out. We'd been given the shaft once again.

Memory Bank Activated: 4-17-1977
Subject: The Nam–1966
Content: Stay-Behind Mission

The men made a lot of extra noise clearing out of the area, banging pots and pans at breakfast, and making sure "Charlie" heard them loading the helicopters. By afternoon, the last of the Bravo company that served as the command post loaded onto the green whirlybirds and left the area. The only thing they left behind was the Recondos. Before daybreak, our platoon had moved out.

With five days' rations, drawn from the supply, we headed into the bushes. For a couple of hours, the line of men moved steadily deeper into the backcountry. After crossing the valley, we came to the source of the tiny stream that began at the base of a small mountain covered with thick brownish-green overgrowth. Stopping to fill the canteens, the lieutenant laid the plan out for us.

After checking out the top of the mountain, we would then secure it and build a perimeter around the only path leading to the top. There, as observers, we'd have a complete view of the valley trails. Again, he emphasized the need for complete silence.

"One cough, one spoken word," he said, "or a rattled pan from a mess kit could cost all of us our lives. There is to be no smoking or striking of matches, nor any cooking at all. We'll only have meals that could be eaten out of the package."

Over the following week, we almost starved to death. Half the rations we were packing needed to be cooked, something we couldn't do. The second day after we occupied the high ground, two companies of North Vietnamese Regulars and their Viet Cong support groups moved in and pitched tents at the base of the mountain. I was awake the full night. In fact, nobody slept.

Their base camp perimeter was about five or six hundred yards below us. We were able to hear sounds they made and could see the edge of their camp from the cliff edge we were using as an observation post. The only thing keeping them from finding out we were there was that they hadn't looked!

We were thinking it was only a matter of time before a squad would be assigned to check out the path leading up the mountain. There was no way they'd miss our positions. Washington was assigned to cover the trail with his M-60 machine gun, along with the gunner from the second squad. We were dug in, camouflaged, and waiting. Nothing happened. That was the hardest part. Sitting on the little mountain for nearly a week without being able to speak above a whisper.

Then suddenly one morning, the noises in their camp increased for a couple of hours, and when we looked, they were gone. We'd watch them run patrols all over the area, except to the top of the mountain where they had set their temporary base camp.

Everybody had run out of water. And not being able to call for a supply airdrop, we needed food as well. So the decision was made to send one squad down to the stream at the foot of the mountain loaded with the canteens from the platoon. The third squad was elected.

Collecting the canteens, we started down the path. Then it hit me. Something was wrong. I was on point! Red had always been on the point until he was killed. Some new guy I didn't know had taken his place. Nobody had given it a second thought, including me. We'd followed the instinctive pattern they taught us. Fall in line in your proper space. Maybe the new guy didn't know that grenadiers never walked point. I didn't want to handle the point with the M-79. I only had one shot. Most point men keep the M-16s they carried on automatic. Even with a shotgun canister, I was in trouble if confronted by more than one man. This left me in a fix.

With the "no talking" rule and the narrow path, it was too late to try and straighten it out. As I'd feared, the worst happened. Turning a sharp bend halfway down the trail, I walked smack into a North Vietnamese Regular. He was just getting ready to make the turn coming up the dirt path. We stood frozen, staring at one another. I could see the sweat dripping down his face. He was only a boy, probably about my age, but he looked young, younger than any soldier I'd ever seen.

His AK-47 was at the high port position with the tip of the barrel next to the left side of his face. The short barrel of the M-79 I was carrying was "business end out." It was aimed at his stomach. Time seemed to stop, but in reality, it was only a split second. I could see the panic on his face, which was in contrast to his slowness to react.

He must be high on opium, I thought.

They carried it around rolled up in little brown balls. The pale tinge in his complexion told me I was right. And in that infinite amount of time, which in actuality lasted a second, I knew if he lowered the barrel of the submachine gun, I would have to kill him.

The barrel of the AK started moving in my direction. Panic grabbed me for the first time, not in fear for myself, but for a mad moment, I wanted desperately to tell him not to try and use the weapon, yet all the time aware that it was too late.

Dropping to one knee, I pulled the trigger. The shotgun blast hit him in the neck and shoulder, spinning him around and knocking him face down in the bushes that lined the trail. I kneeled there; as the new point man came up, I got mad.

"Why the fuck aren't you on point! That's your fucking job, ain't it?"

Sarge came up to the head of the line with Hooper and Clinton. He sent them down the path to see if the soldier had been alone. Coming over to me, he asked if I was okay. All I could do was nod that I was okay.

"Take it easy on the new guy, Ware," he told me. "It's his first time running point."

Then we heard M-16 gunfire down the trail. Clinton and Hooper came running back. There had been two more of them as far as they were able to tell. They got one; the other was wounded but had gotten away. Sarge canceled the forge for water and took us back to the platoon.

The lieutenant decided not to wait for the possible return of the unit the three-man patrol belonged to. Every North Vietnamese soldier in the area had heard the sound of the American weapons. We collected our gear and the whole platoon stopped at the stream, got water, then moved as fast as possible out of the area.

Still, no matter how far we moved away from the side of the mountain, the face of the boy I'd killed stuck in my mind. Why had he done it? If he had just surrendered, he would still be alive. But then the thought struck me, we'd been ordered not to take any prisoners. Still, hadn't he been aware that I didn't want to kill him? Why did he have to lower the weapon?

As we double-timed down the mountain, I kept thinking to myself, *I don't belong here and neither did he, the boy that I had to kill.*

This was not what I was put on this planet for, not for death and destruction. This wasn't what I was all about. I vowed to find a way to get off the line and out of Vietnam, if possible.

Memory Bank Activated: 4-19-1977
Subject: The 'Nam–1966
Content: Wasting the "Papa-Son"

It took three days to force march out of the jungle. What happened on the second day was the thing that upset everybody. A supply drop was ruled out by headquarters. The reason they said, too many "Charlies" in the vicinity. The only way to get more food and ammunition was by walking to a location the supply choppers and gunships could buzz with a reasonable amount of safety.

It took us two days and five different sites before the A-OK came back from the brass. While waiting at the drop location for the sorely needed provisions, the second squad was stationed about fifty yards out in front of the platoon. After half an hour of baking in the sun, everybody was becoming dazed from the heat when the second squad sergeant and a Private first class named Lewis brought in a black pajama-clad Vietnamese. The sergeant pushed him in front of the lieutenant. I was too far away to hear the conversation, but I could see that the "papa-son" was excited, continually speaking the fast clip dialog of

Vietnamese, flinging his hands in expressional gestures, trying to make the American soldiers understand what he was trying to say.

They tied his hands behind his back, then took him down into the ravine that ran next to the well-used path. Murphy, our sniper, who'd been watching the back trail reported to the lieutenant there, then came over by me. He propped the sniper's 30-6 rifle against the base of a small tree and plopped on the ground beside me.

"They're going to kill him," he said, nodding his head toward the men in the ravine. Before I could say anything, I heard loud shouting coming from the trooper named Lewis, breaking the silence we had been living under for the past eight days. Everybody tensed up, reaching for their weapons. Usually, a shout meant trouble on a patrol. Lewis came storming out of the ditch.

"Hell, no! I won't do it! You bastards can go to hell!"

Davis and Hooper both put their fingers to their mouths "shushing" him, trying to keep him quiet. Then the little old man started raising his voice, but before anyone could make a move, the sergeant from the second squad pulled out his Rambo knife and cut his throat. The old man's body jerked in death convulsions. He fell to the ground, clenching his throat trying to stop the bleeding.

Lewis was cussing even more now, this time softly, yet I could feel the emotion in his words. Pulling away from Davis and Hooper, he sat down on the side of the trail. The lieutenant and the sarge from the second squad walked over to him. It wasn't possible to hear all that was said, only the lieutenant telling Lewis that he would be reprimanded for disregarding a direct order.

The sound of the helicopter and the call over the radio broke up the confusion. The supply drop was coming in and had to be picked up. It wasn't until two days later, after we'd returned to base camp, that I found out the whole story. During the reveille formation that morning, Lewis was called out of the ranks. For nearly an hour, he was in the headquarters tent with a board of inquiry. When they came out, Lewis was in the custody of MPs and a young officer. I could tell by his manner and appearance that he was fresh from the States. There was a jeep waiting for them.

The officer made the mistake only a green officer would make in a combat zone. You never, ever try to muscle combat harden veterans. Walking toward the jeep, he gave Lewis a shove to hurry him up. Lewis didn't like it. Turning, he threw all two hundred pounds of his weight into a double-handed, hand-cuffed punch that knocked the second lieutenant on his butt. He lay on the ground, out cold. The two MPs grabbed Lewis before he had a chance to stomp the man.

The captain came out of the headquarters tent. Sending for a medic, he had him take care of the lieutenant, then gave Lewis a dressing down in front of the dozen men who had seen the knockout. He made sure everybody heard that there would be a severe penalty for striking a superior officer added to the charges of disobeying a direct order. Assigning the company's first sergeant to act as an escort, he had them take Lewis away.

SP/4 Boswell was the company clerk and knew all the answers concerning what happened in the battalion. Catching him coming out of H.Q., we crowded around him, prying the information out of him. He told us that the charges against Lewis stemmed from the incident on the trail with the old papa-son. The sergeant from the second squad ordered Lewis to kill him, saying he could have been a Viet Cong. Lewis had refused.

In his statement to the company commander, Lewis said his feelings were the man was an innocent farmer coming back home from a trip to town. He'd searched his belongings and found nothing but a few personal things and a small supply of foodstuffs, which backed up the old man's story; therefore, he felt that killing him was unjustifiable because the man was a civilian and not a member of hostile enemy forces. After hearing the story, we all felt the same way.

After Operation John Paul Jones, things started coming out into the open. A lot of racial tension developed. Confederate flags appeared in the company areas. To counter this, the "Bloods," (Black soldiers) who made up a disproportionate number of the front-line troops, adopted the red, black, and green flags that stood for Black liberation. Fights ensued, and a lot of the Bloods ended up with "bad paper" (Dishonorable Discharges).

In the fall of 1966, it was becoming hard for the combat units to maintain a high degree of morale, especially with Black troops. But unknown to me, back in the States a lot of the Black liberation movements were supported by the "Brotherhood." I was clued in by my old friend, Morris. It was a month after Operation John Paul Jones.

I was riding a two-and-a-half-ton truck on my way to town on one of the six-hour passes they allowed us. Just before turning onto the highway leading into the city, the driver stopped to pick up a marine who was hitchhiking. This wasn't unusual because there were always men from other units and branches of the service traveling back and forth from the harbor down the beach from where the battalion was bivouacked.

Placing the grease gun he carried across his lap, he sat next to the tailgate on the truck. At first, it was the grease gun that held my attention; they were not usually seen in the 'Nam. Then I had a funny feeling that I knew the man. It took a second or two before it dawned on me; it was Morris! He sat there with his chin resting on his chest. Once in a while, he would cast his eyes in my direction. When he was sure I'd recognized him, a smile came over his face.

Memory Bank Activated: 4-20-1977
Subject: The Nam-1966
Content: Rich Man's War-Poor Man's Burden

Everything flooded back to me, the years in Chicago, the Egyptian Cobras. Moving to the back of the truck, I acted like it was his weapon I was interested in.

"Say, brother man, you don't see many pieces like the one you carrying. It works okay in this climate?"

"Works great in all types of weather," he replied. "Like you airborne guys, they keep changing my location." This was a code phrase, meaning it will be necessary for me to stand by for a new assignment. The idea of a change in climate brought a smile to my face. After getting off the truck at the edge of the "strip" (a row of bars that were sanctioned by the U.S. and Vietnamese governments with V.D. shots and condoms included) Morris and I walked down the row of bamboo huts with tin roofs that served as watering holes for G.I.s. The boardwalk was crowded with American and Vietnamese whores.

Tiny shops of various descriptions jammed themselves into the catwalks between the bars. Peddlers constantly put on a hard sell along the narrow walkways. They were mostly young kids and old people trying to sell brightly colored souvenirs or food that the soldiers had been warned not to eat. This gave the place with we called a "Dodge City" cowboy atmosphere.

After going through a block of the shoot 'em up saloons, we finally found one that wasn't too crowded or getting busted up by a drunk G.I. The place was empty except for two soldiers and the girls that worked there. Before we had time to sit down, the girls were on us. One in a red Chinese-style dress thrust her hips in and out, using the term the soldiers taught her for sex.

"Say, soul brother. Me number one girl; you like 'boom, boom?'"

Sending them away, we asked instead for the only cold thing they had, Vietnamese Tiger beer. I was still elated seeing the familiar face of an old friend when the waitress brought the two large brown bottles of strong brew that we soldiers called "Tiger Piss."

Morris hadn't had much to say, neither did I. There weren't many things he could talk about. Where he'd been, what he was doing in 'Nam, and why he was traveling as a marine. All questions I didn't bother to ask.

Within half an hour, the heat became unbearable inside, with the sun beating down on the tin roof. We left, heading into the city of Tuy Hoa. Morris talked a little then, telling me about the "Brotherhood" and what was happening back in the world. Times were changing, and the folks at home began to wake up to the game being played with the lives of Americans and Vietnamese in the war. People had begun to protest and refuse induction into service.

Morris gave me a rundown of the political sellout of the American G.I. and what different organizations in the States were doing to stop the war and expose the corrupt elements in the government.

Stopping for a moment, he interrupted the conversation, as we listen to a trio of Vietnamese street musicians. The string and wind instruments, along with the offbeat rhythm of the oddly shaped round drum, produced the haunting high-pitched sounds I'd so often hear in old Asian movies. Everything else was different here in the Far East, but the music was the same. We watched the old men that stood around the musicians; they seemed to be absorbing the harmony, each one separate, yet a part of the same world. Morris noticed the vibes and turned to me.

"You're right, Brother, that's what we need, more harmony."

He'd always been able to sense what I was thinking without my speaking. Some people are in tune that much. We walked down the street, taking in the sights.

While waiting for a traffic cop to whistle the pedestrians across an intersection, I asked Morris about the master. The mention of his name had an uplifting effect on all the members of the Brotherhood.

"Fine," he said. "I'm beginning to understand what he meant about planning for the future. He asked me to tell you that you are the one; do not die here for an unjust cause. You will be needed by your people later. Be aware! Remember who you are and what your true mission is."

It was becoming harder to keep my sights on what I was supposed to be about, my so-called universal identity. Looking at the signs of war and death that showed up even in the crippled and orphaned kids that ran up to us begging for piasters (Vietnamese money) in the few words of English they'd learned. How could the things that the "Love Section" were supposed to bring about happen in the midst of all this hate and destruction?

Morris saw the look of hopelessness on my face.

"Take it easy, Blood. We know what you've been through here. It's completely against everything the Brotherhood stands for. Yet, if none of the brothers had gotten over here, then none would be going back to tell what is happening here. Remember what the master said; 'we overcome the negative to build on the positive.' Besides, how can you truly know beauty if you have never seen the ugly?"

He knew this type of logic always appealed to me.

"We are a people of paradox," I said. "They call us the bad guys when, in actuality, we're the good guys."

He grinned. "Yeah, it's always been that way. Remember back in Chi-town? Everybody in the neighborhood thought we were a gang of thugs." We both laughed at the memories.

Walking down the cobblestone street watching the people, the war seemed far away. After spending a few hours together, we bid each other farewell. Morris's orders put him on a ship on its way back to the States, although he hinted that was not his destination. I was tempted to ask him how high up in the government and military the Brotherhood could reach, if it could get his orders and mine changed whenever there was a need? Once again, I wanted to go with him, no matter what the cost. Instead, I made it back to camp for the six o'clock formation.

Memory Bank Activated: 4-21-1977
Subject: The Nam - 1966-1967
Content: Coming off the Line

That night, while on guard duty, the opportunity to get off the "combat line" presented itself. A transcendence happened.

I accidentally let it slip to my homeboy Murphy that my eighteenth birthday was coming up, and I wouldn't have been sent to the 'Nam if they'd known my age.

"You should tell them," he said. "It is one way to get off the line. Walking behind the point man gives you what... less than five seconds before you get killed in a firefight? Think about it, baby brother."

Everyone in the squad had started calling me that after Washington jokingly said I looked like his twelve-year-old baby brother.

The next day, the word had spread throughout the squad. Saving each other's lives was priority number one for us combat soldiers. Without my knowledge, the members of the third squad decided to do something about it. Two days later, the summons for my presence came from company headquarters.

Boswell was on the typewriter when I came in; he looked at me with a blank expression on his face. "You only seventeen years old, huh?"

The word had reached H.Q. I just gave a shrug and didn't answer.

Boswell trained his blank stare on the typewriter,

"The captain will see you in a minute."

No matter what the situation, his demeanor never changed. The company's first sergeant appeared at the captain's door.

"Report to Captain Ware."

He had a file and some papers with him. Passing him, I could see the file belonged to me. Giving me "at ease," the Captain leaned back in the swivel chair. He held one of the new battery-powered hand-held fans about six inches from his face. The heat inside any enclosed structure was always warmer than the blistering hot ninety-eight-degree temperature outside. He looked at a copy of my records on his desk. Mainly a paper officer, he was involved in very little combat duty. The headquarters company was exactly that, a headquarters that kept records and supplies, it was the "main office" of the 2nd battalion. Naturally, they would have a businessman running it. Only one problem, I was in the recon platoon. We were the only combat troops in the headquarters company. I wondered if the captain ever had twenty rounds from a Chinese AK-47 coming in his direction? Having seen him out in the field on a few different occasions, I figured he'd seen some action. Did he know the law of the jungle dictates that you must hunt to survive? Hunting means killing. The men online dealt with this ideology on a daily basis.

Recon was close to fifty percent Black, while staff, supply, mail, and the rest of headquarters' units were eighty percent white.

My hunter's instinct told me I was going to get some static. He dropped the fan to his desk.

"P.F.C. Ware, word has reached us that the age listed in your records is not correct. Is that right?"

"Yes, sir," I answered plainly.

"Private Ware, do you realize that for a soldier to participate in this war he must legally be at least eighteen years old?"

"Yes, sir," I answered again.

He picked up the fan, leaning back in the chair.

"Do you have any proof to substantiate this claim?"

"Yes, sir, I do."

Reaching into the slanted top pocket of the jungle fatigues, I handed him a copy of my birth certificate with my real date of birth. He looked at it, then put it in the file on his desk. "Okay, Ware, we'll send this to command and see what they say. You won't be able to go on any more missions until this matter is cleared up. Meantime, you'll still be assigned to the Recondo platoon. The first sergeant will tell you what your duties will be… you're dismissed."

That evening, after six o'clock formation, the first sergeant took me to the rear of the company area. About fifty yards behind the last row of Hootches, were the latrines. Since I wasn't going to "toe" the line and stay on the "combat line," they found the dirtiest, filthiest job they could find for me to do. The job consisted of cleaning out the latrine.

Unfastening the back of the portable outhouses, you had to pull out the cut in half fifty-gallon drums that contained the human waste material of the dozens of men who used the latrine daily. Dragging the two-thirds full drums with a three-foot-long hook to a ditch you had to dig behind the outhouses, you had to pour gasoline on the human manure and set it on fire.

After it had burned satisfactorily, it was to be buried in the pre-dug hole, and a sign stating what was lying only a few inches under the surface was placed on the site. The job lasted one day. After that, I couldn't stand it.

On the second day, one of the barrels exploded, sending a shower of human waste over a forty-yard radius, bringing a dozen armed men running back to see what was happening. When I got to the scene, the first sergeant got on my case.

"Ware, what the hell's going on back here?"

"I don't know, sergeant," I lied. "The handle on the shovel broke when I was digging the hole. I set the barrels on fire and went to the supply tent to turn in the broken shovel and get a new one. That's all I know."

Someone mentioned that it might have been the infiltrators who sometimes slipped in with the Vietnamese workers we hired. They had caught one dropping a grenade in the fire barrel we used outside the headquarters tent to burn important documents. A few of the men had been hit by the shrapnel from the blown apart trash cans. There was a suspicion that some of the Vietnamese workers around the base camp were in actuality, Viet Cong.

When the "shitters," as they were called, exploded two days in a row, they gave me a new job as company mail clerk, and put an armed guard at the latrine.

I was the only man not afraid to take a crap around the company area for nearly a week. Everybody else felt safer utilizing the open countryside.

Due to the hurry-up and wait slowness of military life, it was two weeks before I heard back on the matter of my age. They decided I was to be shipped to Germany, where a brand-new tour of duty would be arranged for me. One lasting for at least a year upon my date of arrival.

It was the end of December, and I'd been in the country since June. With the five months I'd already spent in the 'Nam, that would boost the time spent overseas close to eighteen months instead of the one-year tour of combat duty. The reassignment was optional; I optioned to stop them from shipping me out. When the captain asked me to sign the request, I said no. I wanted to finish out the last seven months left on my tour. There was nothing they could do. Since I was only seventeen years old, they weren't able to put me back online until after my birthday, which was a month and a half away. I figured this would give me about two more months of "ghost time" as we called it, time not spent in the boonies, bringing me closer to my rotation date, giving me a better chance to survive, and make it back to the States.

There are signs given to us by things that happen around us. One of these signs was given to me shortly after coming out of the boonies.

The young Black brother from New York City who took my spot in the third squad was killed. His first name was George. Like many of the small details of what happened, his last name fails to register in my memory bank. Only the presence of the man has remained fully intact. If I hadn't "ghosted" off the line, there was a possibility of my being the one who caught the bullet. I'd had to brief George when he'd first came to the squad. It wasn't until after his death that I found out why I got heavy vibrations of some kind of kinship when we first met. I thought the underlying message was that he was taking my place among the men I looked upon as my brothers. At times, the ability to forecast and receive vibrations can be very puzzling.

I'd had the feeling he was dead when I saw the helicopters bring the platoon in from the fields. Vietnam taught me to accept the things I "felt," as things that will usually come about. I have no doubt that George's death was also meant as a sign to me. A sign directing me to finish the real task I was put here on earth to perform. One thing was for sure, I wasn't going back online for a while.

The month and a half I'd hoped for turned into two. It was one time the slowness of military bureaucracy worked for me instead of against me.

The 101st had been moving quite a bit since the Christmas holidays. Operations took us from Tuy Hoa back to Kon-Tum, near the borders of Laos and Cambodia, where we stayed for a month. Then the battalion returned to Phan-Rang, the division base camp.

Patrols were run in conjunction with the Royal Korean Marines that manned the perimeter and cleared the countryside of V.C. Phan-Rang was a picnic compared to some of the places we'd been.

Most of my time was divided between sorting mail for the platoons in the company and free time to check out the city and learn some of the customs. The first of March came, bringing a return of the monsoons. Now the platoon was moving out again, going back to the boonies. But not me, I was going to Taipei, Taiwan. My five-day R and R had come through.

Memory Bank Activated: 4-22-1977
Subject: Sammy Chung
Content: Taipei, Taiwan

In the late sixties, they called it "Free China." It looked like New York, Chicago, and Los Angeles all rolled into one and crowded on a tiny island off the coast of Mainland China. This colorful land with its bright ornaments held the answers to many questions for me. It was there I met "Little Sammy Chung" and Jomo, a native of Africa.

A surprise bonus had fallen into my lap. The route taken by the aircraft required they make a thirty-minute layover in Hong Kong. Due to an engine maintenance snafu, it was stretched to six hours. That gave us a chance to tour the buzzing metropolis. When I got to the city of Taipei, it was set up the same way: all hustle and bustle.

After leaving the briefing the R & R officer gave me, I left the depot and was almost run over by a bright red streak that turned out to be a taxi. Watching the traffic flow, I was doubtful about taking the offered ride. I'd never seen anything move as fast as the traffic in this city. After spending nine months in the jungle, the pace of a large city seemed to have doubled to me. My eyes and other sensory organs couldn't absorb everything they were getting from the neon lights, crowded streets, and the honking horns of the automobiles. The driver, honking the horn of the compact taxi, leaned over the seat, and opened the door on the passenger side.

"Come on, get in, friend.

"You like jazz, don't you? I know just the place you want to go to."

He rapped a better line than most hustlers I'd met on the streets in America.

Getting into the back seat, I took out the piece of paper in my back pocket that had the names and addresses of the hotels the R & R officer said were best for G.I.s to get a room. The driver, watching the traffic, turned the wheel sharply and shot the red buzz bomb into an empty slot in the rapidly moving non-stop stream of cars.

Without looking back, he said, "You can put that away. The best hotel for a Brother is the Golden Dragon."

Vibrations tingled in the atmosphere. I became more attentive to what he was saying.

"Where did they tell you to go, the Ambassador or The Grand?"

"Yeah, that's the game they run. A lot of them get a kickback for steering G.I.'s on R & R to those clip joints. They know you've saved some money to enjoy yourself during the five days they've given you. You want to relax from the horrors you've been through."

"Don't sweat it, my man, we'll show you lots of 'Brotherhood' while you are here."

There was that word… Brotherhood. The vibrations were strong. Who was this guy I wanted to know?

I began to ease back into the seat, becoming used to the faster pace of the modern surroundings of this world-class city. I got the feeling that I was about to get into something beyond rest and relaxation. The car came to a screeching halt, and the traffic stream stopped in mid-flight. Looking over his shoulder, the driver flashed a grin.

"Oh, by the way, my name is Sammy Chung. All the Brothers call me Little Sammy."

My vibrations had been right. I'd been picked for some kind of assignment again.

"My name is Billy," I said.

We shook hands. As quickly as it had stopped, the traffic resumed its maddening rush to nowhere. Five minutes later, we pulled in front of a hotel with the mouth of a golden dragon framing the heavy glass doors. The building was on a sloping hill, and next to it was a lounge with a red dragon's mouth framing its small entrance.

Sammy got out of the car, and taking the suit bag and shaving kit from me, he gave them to a teenage boy that came out of the glass doors.

"This is my younger brother." Sammy playfully slapped the kid on the back.

"Come on, I'll take you in to register; then we'll go over to the Red Dragon for a while."

Memory Bank Activated: 4-24-1977
Subject: Jomo the Wise
Content: Taipei, Taiwan

After taking a quick shower to freshen up, I took the elevator down to the lobby. Sammy was waiting for me at the main desk. Still not sure if he had an assignment for me, or even if he was a member of the "Brotherhood," I figured it wasn't going to take long to find out one way or the other.

Next door at the bar, Sammy moved like a whirlwind, ordering drinks for us while talking to the bartender and a girl who occupied the lounge that he said he managed for his father, who owned the hotel and the adjoining lounge. Sitting at one of the tables, I was enjoying the simple luxury of having ice cubes in my drink, something I hadn't experienced for half a year.

Sammy started digging for a little background information with the leading question asked of war veterans.

"You got that look, what do they call it…the thousand-yard stare? You must have seen a lot of combat during your time in Vietnam, huh?"

I gave him a shrug and replied, "More than I needed to."

The last thing I wanted to talk about was 'Nam and the war. He shook his head as if he understood how I felt.

"Hold on a minute, there's another Brother that's staying here. I'd like you to meet him." Disappearing into the back, he came out with a different "type" of Black man.

It shocked me at first. I'd expected he meant another American. I could tell by the way he was dressed and his dark complexion that he was an African.

I was staring at him, unable to stop, as Sammy brought him over to the booth. Sammy made the introductions in his perfect English.

"Billy, this is Yusuf, a friend, and one of our Brothers from Central Africa. He wants to talk to you about something very important, to his people back home, and to the Brotherhood."

Yusuf gave me a slight nod that most Africans used when meeting strangers. Sitting across from me at the table, he became quiet, not quite sure how to begin. Sammy could see things were awkward.

"I'll let you two get to know each other." He walked away.

I waited for the man to speak.

"Well, Billy, you are an American soldier, right?" He seemed to be trying to remember information about me.

"On leave from Vietnam; yes?"

I sat there soberly, nodding my head, waiting for the punch line to fall. He continued. "I met another American a few days ago," he said.

He was trying to check me out and possibly win my confidence at the same time.

"Oh," I said, showing interest, "and where was he from in America?"

"Chicago, but he travels all over the world…yes quite a bit, actually."

Vibrations had already told me the answer. I asked anyway.

"What was his name?"

"Morris," he answered in his Afro-British accent.

I stared into his eyes, trying to read the man, but there was no connection. I waited for him to make the next move, but he was silent. Maybe he wasn't the one with the message for me. I thought, okay, I'll cut to the chase.

I asked him, "What do you want me to do?"

He seemed surprised, but relieved, and he relaxed a little.

"There is someone Morris wants you to talk to and help them to take care of a problem. Morris says you must decide that you want to do this on your own. It is most dangerous and will require a small amount of your time."

I thought about Vietnam and the valleys of death I'd been walking thru for the past half a year.

"Where do we have to go?" I wanted to know. "My time is limited. I've only got five days here."

Waving to Sammy, who was talking to the girl at the end of the bar, he called him over. Sammy assured me that it wouldn't take up much of my time. The man I was to meet could fill me in on the details, and how important the matter was.

Sammy drove us in the red buzz bomb. Most of the cars in the high-powered traffic were compact and were painted red, which gave the vehicles the feeling of one long mechanical entity. The faster the traffic moved, the faster everything else moved in the city. Even the people seemed to move at the pace of the little red cars as I watched them hurrying down the sidewalk. The oddity of the traffic pattern and bright neon signs was still playing havoc with my visual and audio senses. Taipei is one of the fastest-moving cities in the Far East. Sammy safely maneuvered us through the heart of downtown, past the government buildings and the United States military complexes.

Coming to the bay area, we moved slowly down to the dock and stopped at a Lebanese freighter tied to the wharf. Yusuf led me up the gangplank and onto the deck of the ship. There were three men standing there; I expected men of darker complexions than the ones we met. The one in the middle with the captain's hat was a blue-eyed blonde. My guard went up. At first, a warning flashed in my head, but the warm greeting between Yusuf and the men helped to dispel my suspicions. He introduced us, using the phrases of the Brothers and the captain gave me the handshake of the Brotherhood.

Taking me to one of the lower deck cabins, Yusuf asked me to wait while he knocked softly at the door. He and the captain entered the unusually plush stateroom. Emerging a few seconds later, he asked me to please go in.

Stepping into the room, the vibrations became tremendous. It looked like the stateroom of an African king. I took a glance around, knowing they didn't want me here to appraise the furniture. My eyes fell on the man sitting in the high-back upholstered chair. The first thing I noticed was his regal bearing. There seemed to be an "aura" about him, topped off by his thick, gray hair. He was clean-shaven, wearing a light green two-piece Nehru suit, similar to the ones worn by the Chinese and Indian leaders on the mainland. The "aura" around him was one of wisdom, patience, and experience.

Without saying a word, he gestured to the davenport built into the bulkhead of the cabin. Sitting down, I waited for him to speak, feeling out of place making the first move.

"Your name is Billy, not Bill, or William, is it not?" He had a rich voice, and his accent was slightly less than Yusuf's.

"Yes, that's right," I answered.

"Well, Billy, my real name is not important, and it is probably better if you do not know it. My Brothers call me Jomo. We have a mutual friend who thought you might be able to help us."

He got up and walked over to the portal, looking out into the darkness.

"He was to do the job himself," he continued, "but was called away on another, no doubt more pressing, matter." "He was able, however, to find out that your leave orders bring you here to the city of Taipei at a most auspicious time, and time is critical at this juncture."

He turned and came back and stood a few feet in front of me.

"Our mutual friend explained to me that you are not of the "guerilla faction" of the Brotherhood, but you come from a newly formed faction called 'Love Section.' Is that correct?"

"Yes…" I started to answer, but he had turned away, lost in his own thoughts.

"An unusual name for such an advanced concept," he said to himself as he walked back and resumed staring out the closed portal.

Without looking at me, he asked me what my duties were as a soldier in Vietnam. I told him about the Recondo platoon and the search and destroy missions. After listening to me, he came and sat beside me and changed the subject.

"Yusuf and the captain tell me you seem to be distrustful of people who are not Black."

I shrugged, not quite knowing how to answer the question. Then I thought better of it. I had reacted to the captain and crew just as any combat vet would have when approaching new situations and people; that was with caution.

Jomo picked up on my vibes. "Most soldiers are jumpy and suspicious for a while after coming out of combat," he said.

Then he turned very serious. "The captain of the ship is white, Sammy is yellow, you are brown, and I am Black. The 'Brotherhood of Men' extends beyond the basis of skin color or nationality. We are here to bring about one ideology and the members of the "Love Section" are the reasons we who wear the "mask of the guerilla" fight the battles today in a more traditional way. You have been chosen as a special liaison between the different factions of the Brotherhood. That was the reason you have been sent into the 'valley of death' here in Asia. From what you have experienced, you must teach others that know nothing of the existence of the death and destruction that will come to them out of hatred and war." He leaned closer.

"I have been told that this is your mission."

He stood and started pacing in front of me as he talked.

"The valley of death is never stationary nor confined to theaters of war and warriors. Greedy men manipulate its location, causing it to move across the face of the planet and consume those seeking freedom as well. We are experiencing it at home… our home. Yes, Africa is your home. The land from which your fathers were stolen. You have been taught the knowledge of how this happened and why. You know who is responsible. Many of your peers do not. They have not been told of the forces working against them, for these very forces are skilled in the arts of concealing knowledge and replacing it with doctored propaganda. They use this propaganda to breed distrust and a lack of cooperation between us. That is why you may ask, 'Why should I do this thing, they ask me to do?' You may even say, America, not Africa, is my home!" He chuckled.

"I have been to America, and heard these words spoken by the Black people there, and they are my brothers. Are we not from the same land, the same generic womb? Black people in America have been led to believe Africa is a land of wild beasts and even wilder people. The children of the ones who stole your mothers and fathers, taking them to the Americas, also lied to you about the true nature of your homeland have followed the misguided teachings of their fathers. They seek to keep a stolen Africa; the very land they tell you is useless. Does a sane man steal a useless thing? Africa is rich in land and natural resources and belongs to the African people. Africa belongs to you also, young Brother, and she has need of you."

"Trust me," he continued. "Close your eyes for a moment."

I closed my eyes, listening to his voice that sounded almost hypnotizing as he spoke.

"Because you were kidnapped and held in bondage for hundreds of years does not mean your home is not still your home."

Transcending began for me as I let his words enter my mind. The room dissolved, and his words took me to the geological center of Africa. It was the first time I'd transcended through time and space and became a part of the experiences of another person.

Standing on a large mountain, I was able to see the entire continent. There he showed me the land from which I came, and the garden in which I'd lived.

"Behold." Jomo pointed his hand to the sky. The wind rushed past us, pushing clouds by, blowing them across the green valleys.

Jomo's gray hair bristled with a sparkling kind of glow as he stood beside me.

"Look into the valleys. Can you not see the great resources? You come from the most bountiful land on Mothership Earth."

The entire universe came rushing at me. Traveling into space, worlds passed below me, planet after planet. I had never transcended to such a point. It began to disturb me. The feeling of not being able to reverse the transformation crept over me. I was picking up too much information.

Each world that I passed sent tremendous vibrations at me. Vibrations contain their life forms, ways, customs, and habits.

Forcing myself, I relaxed, taking deep breaths and willing myself to the present, the here, the now. Slowly, the room came into focus. The transformation had taken place in less than thirty seconds.

Jomo was still talking. "Come here. There is something I want to show you."

Taking me to the portal, he showed me a medium-sized Portuguese freighter across the harbor. Jomo put his hand on my shoulder.

"That ship is on its way to the continent of Africa. There is a ton of munitions and equipment it is carrying that will be unloaded in a neutral seaport, along with one hundred and three mercenaries it is picking up from various countries. This load of equipment and ammunition will be transported by direct military convoy to South Africa, into Rhodesia, then funneled into the heart of the Congo, which is the present location of the African struggle. There, these mercenaries will use this shipment of arms to kill and suppress my people."

"This new Love Section you are in..." he said, as we walked back and sat down.

"… I am doubtful of its effectiveness in the stage of struggle my people are in today." "Possibly, in the future, we can use this type of philosophy to bring all humanity into unity, but right now, what is needed are the talents you have learned in Vietnam. As you have been told, it is a very dangerous thing we ask you to do. You will have to put your life at risk. I have been told of the contradiction under which you exist. The Brothers on the council of elders said the choice must be yours to make."

Memories of some of my earlier teachings dominated my thoughts. For a moment, we sat in silence. Thoughts of earlier meditations came back to me. I closed my eyes for a brief second, reciting to myself what always centered me, enabling me to look beyond the materialistic world.

To be. Simply, to be. And be aware, is the essence of all creation.

To be, without the need of substance or body.

To be, without the want of material possessions or the desires created by them.

To exist as part of the whole, nothing has been created that is not connected to all.

With the transformation trip to my genealogical home still fresh in my mind.

"What do you need me to do?" I said.

Jomo sat down in the plush chair. "You are familiar with handling explosives, are you not?"

"To a degree," I answered. "It depends on the kind of explosives you're talking about. If they're American military types, there shouldn't be any problem."

"Then I think you will be able to help us." He seemed pleased with my answer.

He rang a small bell on the table next to his chair. Yusuf entered the room moments later.

"Begin the arrangements," he told him. "Our young Brother has agreed to help us."

He beckons me to the table, spreading out a construction map of the dock area.

"My friend," he said, "that ship must not reach the coast of Africa."

After an hour's briefing, I left the ship.

Resting on the car's fender, Sammy was waiting for me on the dock. Jomo had told me Sammy and two others would be my backup team.

Giving me a high sign, he watched me coming down the gangplank and get in the taxi as I climbed in the back. Looking in the rearview mirror, he could see it on my face; the mission was a go.

"Kind of heavy action, huh?" He started the car.

"Yeah," I said. He chuckled and drove off into the night.

The next day, Sammy roused me out of the sack at daybreak. I'd hated to miss even one of the five days of leave, but time had to be spent in preparation for the coming mission. I got a chance to see another side of Sammy's personality. He was a martial artist of remarkable skill. More extraordinary was his respect for the traditions of the arts. We spent most of the day working out in a Kung-Fu school that was also owned by a member of Sammy's family. There, I met the other two men that would make the raid with us. They were fighters trained in the Wing Chun style of Kung-Fu.

Sammy was surprised I'd received as little training as ten hours of hand-to-hand combat. Living in "Chi-town" had taught me a few street fighting techniques, and I'd picked up some boxing skills at Archie Moore's Chicago gym in the Golden Gloves program.

In Vietnam, I carried a weapon all the time. The only contact with the martial arts had been a couple of hours spent with the Royal Korean Marines that practiced their "Taekwondo" while bivouacking next to our headquarters at Phan-Rang.

We only had a couple of hours, so Sammy showed me some basic fighting techniques like protecting my body's "Four Corners" as he called it, with the "Immovable Elbow Theory" and how to deliver a compact, powerful punch with a low kick to an attacker's legs.

Ending the lesson, his advice was for me to spend a couple of years with him at the school in order to get a good knowledge of the basics.

At about one o'clock, Sammy called a halt. We went back to the hotel and had lunch, then I went upstairs to meditate and prepare for the night. Just before dark, the clerk at the desk called my room.

"The taxi you ordered is waiting for you, sir."

"Okay," I said, "I'll be right down."

Putting on the beige jacket to cover the black body shirt, I took the black ski cap and gloves and stuffed them into the grip bag on top of the explosives Yusuf had given to me. Taking the elevator to the lobby, I met Sammy at the main desk.

"You ready to go?" he asked.

I nodded a yes. His cheerful attitude had vanished. He was all business.

Driving over to the gym, we picked up his two partners, then headed for the docks. It was dark when we got there.

Pulling the car to a halt, we stopped a short distance from the gate entrance to the warehouses on the dock. Sammy killed the lights, and we sat there, watching the building that was between us and the Portuguese freighter.

After a couple of minutes, Sammy decided it was time to go in. Putting on the ski mask and gloves, I took the package of C-4 explosives and slipped the strap over my shoulder, then got out of the car. I couldn't shake the feeling that I'd never left 'Nam.

Memory Bank Activated: 4-28-1977
Subject: Taipei, Taiwan
Content: Blow for Freedom

Climbing the wire mesh fence, we made our way to the back of the warehouse. Sammy had one of the men jimmy open the square-shaped window that faced the back of the building. We shimmied through the opening. Most of the cargo had been loaded onto the freighter, giving the warehouse a hollow, empty look.

After checking out the front of the building, we slowly crept out of the open bay doors onto the dock and crouched behind the large cargo crates stored there. There were four men by the gangplank of the ship, smoking and talking. Sammy's job was to get me past them and onto the ship.

Sammy told me to go back into the warehouse. There was a door at the other end that would put me on the other side of the four men and closer to the gangplank. When I heard the commotion Sammy and the guys were supposed to start, I was to make for the gangplank. I'd already been briefed on the location where they wanted me to plant the charges.

Making my way to the door, I crouched in the semi-darkness. I could hear the men in front of the ship. Peeping out of the dirty windowpane in the door, I could see the men's shadows on the dock lights cast on the concrete.

Within a couple of seconds, I heard the men shouting, running to the other end of the warehouse. Relying on the guards to have gone to investigate the noise, I slipped out the door. Seeing that no one was near the gangplank, I ran up to the railing of the ship, glad for the black clothes they'd given me.

Stepping onto the ship, I headed for the passageway that led down to the cargo level where the munitions were being kept. The information they had given me was correct. The ship seemed to be empty. There were supposed to be less than a dozen men aboard, the rest on leave ashore.

Making my way down into the lower levels of the ship, I carefully avoided the cabins and quarters that would house the crew members. Time seemed to stretch to eternity; the farther I went into the ship, the more isolated I felt. A minute after entering, I found the yellow door with the red warning sign stenciled on it. "Danger-Explosives." Taking the container of acid solution from the demolition kit I was carrying, I poured the metal-eating liquid into the lock of the door. Fumes and smoke poured from the keyhole. I wondered what the flask that contained the stuff was made of, and why it was impervious to the solution? What would have happened if the flask of deadly chemicals had spilled while I was carrying the kit bag? Dismissing the thought from my mind, I gently pushed on the large metal door. The lock popped open, and the door swung on its hinges, crashing against the wall.

Pulling the Browning Mark 1 British pistol from its holster, I froze, sure the racket had been heard. I kept thanking Sammy for the gun that was identical to the M-1911 cal.45 I carried in 'Nam.

Nothing happened, so I went into the storage compartment. Picking out the crates that contained some form of explosives, I went about the business of molding the C-4 demolition charges, putting in detonators and splicing the wires of the three charges into one lead, which I attached to the timing device, setting it for fifteen minutes.

I pulled the door closed and got the hell out of there. When I got back on deck, I could hear the sounds of the fighting on the dock. Stopping at the gangplank and peeping over the railing, I saw that Sammy and his buddies were getting down with the four men that had been guarding the ship. I'd never seen anything like it. It was something out of the martial arts movies I'd seen. "Everybody was Kung-Fu fighting!"

For a split second, I watched the punching and kicking. My guys had been instructed to hit and run, to drag the fight out as long as possible in order to give me time to set my charges.

Little Sammy was fast as lightning! He'd told me earlier that it had a lot to do with practice and timing. Now I saw what he meant. The guy he was fighting was twice his size. Somehow, he managed to grab Sammy's arm. Flipping backward, Sammy landed on his feet and drove a foot into the man's groin. The big guy bent over in pain. Sammy hit him with a salvo of blows to the face. They were so fast I couldn't count them. The giant fell like a freshly cut tree. It was obvious the guards were no match for the trained fighters.

I was enjoying the action on the dock, but it left me with a problem. I could hear the men outside the captain's cabin above my head who were watching the fight. It was imperative that I not be seen. If they caught me on the ship, they could possibly find the storage room broken into and the charges I'd set. I couldn't go down the gangplank without being seen. There wasn't much time before the charges I'd set would go off. Then one of the guards started blowing a whistle he carried. I heard men coming down the metal steps from the captain's cabin.

Moving down the railing toward the bow of the ship, I unsnapped the cover to one of the lifeboats and slipped inside. Voices came from everywhere, calling out in Portuguese. The captain was trying to find out what was happening. Footsteps ran past me, heading for the gangplank. Looking at the fluorescent dial on my watch in the darkness of the lifeboat, my heart began pounding. Three and a half of the fifteen minutes had passed!

To hell with this, I thought. *I'm getting out of here!*

Yanking the cover off the lifeboat, I was surprised to see one of the crew coming toward me. As I climbed out of the lifeboat, he tried to grab me. Instinctively, I used the blocking technique I'd learned earlier in the day and did the short kick to his left knee. When he bent over to grab his knee from the pain, I drove my thigh into his face. He fell on his side and put his hands to his mouth moaning. I believe the blow had broken his jaw.

Seizing the opportunity, I ran to the line at the bow of the ship used to tie her to the dock. The guards on watch had been joined by three other men. This time, the fight didn't interest me. Hooking my arms and legs around the thickly woven rope, I jumped over the side half sliding, half crawling down the fifty odd feet to the mooring below. I hadn't prepared for the impact of landing; it sent shocks of pain throughout my body as I hit the post and dropped to the ground.

Forcing my legs to react, I limped into the warehouse and crawled out the back window. I'd just closed the door of the taxi when Sammy and the rest of the crew came running up. Sammy jumped behind the wheel. Throwing the car into reverse, he did a 180-degree turn, speeding away into the night.

"Well, how did it go?" Sammy asked.

I was in a lot of pain and tried to catch my breath. Before I could answer, we heard the explosion from the waterfront and felt the shockwave. Looking in the rearview mirror, Sammy smiled.

"I guess that answers my question."

He slowed the taxi down as we looked back at the flames, listening to secondary explosions and what sounded like a major battle being fought at the dock. It shook up the whole island. Everyone thought Mainland China was invading.

A few hours later, Yusuf came up to my room at the hotel. He thanked me for Jomo, who had set sail earlier that evening. Wishing me well, he informed me that all my expenses during my stay would be taken care of and that I would find that Africa would be a welcoming place for a Brother like me. He also stressed the need for secrecy about my involvement in the entire matter.

The rest of my time in Taipei was spent doing what I had come for in the first place, rest and relaxationn. The island was locked down for two days while they investigated the incident at the dock, classifying it as the worst accident in the history of the docks, and how come a ship's cargo that dangerous ended up port side and not on record? The investigation was short; they said that the ship had been carrying fertilizer that had gotten ignited by an electrical fire. I bought champagne for Sammy and the team as they interpreted the local news for me. I don't speak Chinese.

Sammy showed me around the city and was instrumental in introducing me to some of the most beautiful women I've ever met. Because of my love of music, especially jazz, he turned me onto the hottest spots on the island. I would sit for hours listening to the musicians. After a couple of days, he gives me a nickname, "Funky Billy Kid." He was always laughing at my habit of following the group and drumming out the musical notes on the tabletop.

Unable to convince him I couldn't stay in Taipei, on my last day, he took me to the airport. Saying goodbye, I regretted leaving, knowing I'd never see him again. Sammy sensed this feeling of loss as well. As he drove away, I thought about the night Little Sammy Chung and Funky Billy Kid had taken on the bad guys and everybody was "Kung-Fu" fighting.

Memory Bank Activated: 4-29-1977
Subject: Vietnam, 1967
Content: Back on Line

The 'Nam was the same old, same old. Only one thing had changed. A third of the battalion was shot up in a renewed battle with units of the 95th and 45th North Vietnamese Regulars.

Jumping from the three-fourth-ton truck that supplied the ride from the airstrip, I stopped to look the place over, not being familiar with this new section of the country. As usual, we were in a thick jungle. It was always thick. The jungle, the fighting.

The death was thick; it lasted forever. You can't get over it, you can't go under it, you can't get around it.

I still carried some of the business cards Davis had ordered half a year ago. Widow Makers, that's what we called ourselves. Was that what I was supposed to be? The four hundred dollars a month pay had seemed small when I first heard that was the amount of pay for Airborne troopers with my rank in a combat zone. What I'd done in Taipei was for free, and it was the only time I was glad to commit an act of violence.

Looking at the road sign, I tried to decipher the name of the hamlet we were bivouacked next to. Unable to figure out the writing of the Vietnamese, I started making my way through the tents, looking for the five-o-deuce. Walking around, I could see that something was up. Everybody was packing field gear or unloading supplies.

Finally finding the company area, I went to the headquarters tent to report back from the Rest & Relaxation I'd just enjoyed. Before I could enter the tent, the captain, first sergeant, and a major I'd never seen before came out.

I came to attention, without saluting; they had asked us not to because it made the officers a target for snipers or infiltrators. The major pointed at me.

"What about him?" The captain said, "Well, sir, he's kind of an unusual case. He was with the recon platoon until we found out he was only seventeen years old."

Vibrations told me what was happening. There had been a heavy firefight. They were pulling everybody from the rear echelon out into the field. The major put on the hard-core act and read the captain out.

"We need every man possible in the field! This is a combat-experienced man, and we can't afford to waste his talents."

Turning to me, he added, "Pack your gear, trooper, and be at the battalion landing zone in thirty minutes!"

They hurried on their way, searching for more replacements. I used the relaxation tactics I'd been taught to calm myself. Most of the men who had less than 90 days left in the country had been given other duties besides combat. They were considered "short-timers," meaning their time in Vietnam had nearly come to an end. With sixty days to go, I was so short that I had to pull myself up by my boot laces.

Building myself up for the trip back into combat, I went in the tent and reported back in to the company. Then I went to the supply tent to pick up my gear and draw rations.

Since Boswell didn't know I was no longer a mail clerk, he asked me to pick up the bundle of letters for the headquarters company. I give him a thumbs-up. When you were out online, a letter from home was better than any stimulant in the world. The men deserved to have their letters now, not two weeks later. Besides, some of the mail was mine.

Packing the things I'd need in the boonies, I took a minute to read one of the letters that belonged to me. It was from my sister, Delores. Reading it gave me a sense of helplessness. In it, she practically begged me not to stay overseas.

I'd written and told them that I might ask for duty in one of the neutral Asian countries until my time was up in the service. In her letter, she mentioned her now ex-husband, Thomas Manning. She had finally filed for a divorce.

There was a problem. Manning had been charged with sales of heroin and Delores received a subpoena to testify since they were no longer married. Tommy had threatened her, telling her what he would do if she testified. Reading the letter my mind raced for a way to get back to the world as soon as possible.

"Ware, you in there?"

It was the first sergeant, standing outside the mail hooch.

"Come on, get a move on. That chopper leaves in five minutes!"

I gave him a "Yo, Sargent" and heard his footsteps crunching on the twigs and branches that covered the company area. Folding the letter, I put it in the waterproof plastic bag along with my wallet.

Slipping my arms through the shoulder straps of my rack sack, I checked my weapon. I'd been issued one of the new experimental XM148 over and under M-16 and M-79 combinations. They had combined the grenade launcher with the automatic rifle. The cocking mechanism was different and so was the site on the weapon. I tried to get familiar with it as I walked to the landing zone. Seven minutes later, we were airborne, heading for the D.M.Z.

Memory Bank Activated: 5-1-1977
Subject: Viet Nam 1967
Content: Agent Orange

My watery eyes were burning. I could smell the chemicals in the air surrounding me. Clinton was the first to realize what was happening,

"Weedkiller!" He squeezed the word out, trying to keep his voice low, and spit the taste out of his mouth.

We all hear them in the distance as they flew in, thinking they were maybe transporting C-130s delivering supplies to one of our bases. When they started coming in low and the chemicals began falling like raindrops of the tree leaves and overhead canopy of vines, it confirmed everybody's fears. We were being sprayed with Agent Orange. Recon platoon was "sneaking a peek" at V.C. locations, which means we dropped into hostile territory without anyone knowing about it.

The Air Force planes overhead were part of "Operation Ranch Hand." They sprayed an area to make a landing zone in preparation for bringing in troops one to two weeks later. They never even knew we were there.

Tears ran down my cheeks, looking up, trying to catch a glimpse of the planes; I felt the drops of oily liquid as they fell into my left nostril. Everybody took out their canteens, trying to wash the stuff off their faces.

We were on another recon special mission that had started two days earlier. We'd been choppered to a location about ten klicks away, then as quietly as possible, hiked to the designated coordinates.

What we didn't know was that there was a tunnel complex along our route. The day before getting sprayed, the V.C. had trapped us in the ambush they'd set up, guarding the trail leading into the complex. Sarge formed us in a fire perimeter, covering both sides of the trail. They had us pinned down pretty good. We were in deep shit.

Lucky for us, an army of South Vietnam detachment (ARVANs) under Special Forces control walked into the set-up from the other side, giving us and the Viet Cong a surprise. It took an hour or so to clear the area, but by then, everyone within twenty klicks knew we were there.

We found one of their field radios that had been shot up by us, so it'd been abandoned by the V.C. We knew the word had been sent out about us.

Sarge formed us up, and we had hit the trail again. Our orders were to rendezvous for extraction. We were needed at other coordinates. It was on that stroll through the jungle we got doused with Agent Orange. My nose and lungs ached from the toxic chemicals.

Everybody complained about headaches, hot flashes, and a feeling like they were itchy with a skin rash. I felt like my chest and head were burning up. There was a unanimous belief that the symptoms were from the weedkiller. We could smell it on everything we carried. I wondered if Charlie would be able to smell us coming. I wanted to find a creek or stream and jump in it with all my gear! I tried to think of something else. The new guys in the third squad, I hadn't had time to get their names! I looked over my shoulder at the man behind me.

Jesus Christ! He looked like he was still in high school. I tried to get a glimpse of the new point man walking a few yards ahead of me as he followed the sharp left turn on the trail. He disappeared behind the large tree beside the bend in the path. Three seconds later, I started making the turn around the tree when *BOOM!*

The explosion blows me off my feet into the air, sending me flying back across the narrow trail and up against a small tree on the other side of the path, knocking the wind out of me. It felt like I'd been hit with a giant two-by-four that covered my whole body. The sudden stop when I hit the tree brought more pain. I think the only thing that saved me from a broken back was my rut sack and its contents. I fell forward, landing and twisting my left ankle. Then my knees hit the ground. Next came the sharp pain in my left wrist; the hand I was carrying my weapon in got jammed between my falling body and the ground. I collapsed face-first on the ground.

The new point man was much worse off than I was. He was only a couple of feet away from the blast, taking the full impact. The tripwire booby trap was a (HE) concussion grenade, used mainly to send out an overpressure shockwave blast. We used them to destroy underground tunnels. He was the second point man I'd lost on my tour.

There was no way for a dust-off helicopter to pick his body up. They brought in a helicopter (HFRS) insertion and extraction crew that just happen to be nearby; they dropped a line and cage through the jungle canopy and took the body out.

They didn't have room to take me. Since there were no visible signs of injury, I had to "ground-pound" it out, "humping the boonies" as we called it, for the next three days before we got to an LZ and were lifted out. I'd never been in that much pain in my life.

Back at base camp, the doctors checked me out and said there was maybe some damage from the blast to my joints, and some of them seemed slightly misaligned (whatever the hell that meant), a mild concussion, and no internal damage to my organs. They could find no broken bones, and since I'd walked across the jungle for three days, everything must be okay. They give me forty-eight hours of bed rest, then I was to return to duty. Two days later, I was back in the field.

Charlie was playing a hit-and-run game with us. This went on for the next two weeks. We'd been flown to the D.M.Z., along the border between North and South Vietnam.

The Battalion was involved in heavy fighting in the area, and casualties were high. Recon was sent to reinforce the Special Forces camp and beef up their firepower. The camp was a training base for the Montagnard and was under siege from across the D.M.Z. The task of securing the base for the Green Berets was given to recon. For several days, we waited out the numerous air strikes called into the surrounding terrain to stop the NVA's advance. Then patrols were mounted to mop up any Viet Cong and NVA left in the countryside. This should have been a normal operation, but it wasn't.

The soaking with Agent Orange and Charlie's strange tactics didn't pan out like the regular search and destroy missions we conducted. Hit-and-run tactics by the Viet Cong were nothing new. But these were North Vietnamese Regulars, near their own home ground. Something was wrong if they weren't putting up a fight.

After a week of the hide-and-seek game, the operation seemed to be a waste of time. With many signs of activity in the jungle, we know they were there, but we had not been able to find them.

That next week, things began to happen. One morning, while on patrol, all of a sudden, the Montagnard guide and the point man froze in front of me. Sensing that something was wrong, I clicked the safety of my weapon. It was quiet, too quiet. Walking slowly up to them, I could see the space opened up into what appeared to be a small clearing. It looked peaceful enough, yet the hairs on the nape of my neck began to rise.

Looking the clearing over, I began to see that some of the vegetation didn't blend with the location, and piles of twigs and branches had been placed around the base of several trees. Suddenly, one of the piles of dead leaves came alive with the muzzle flash of automatic weapons fire. We'd walked into a hidden company base camp.

They were dug into the tunnels, which gave them an advantage. The Montagnard guide was the first to get it. When the bullets hit him, his blood was spread all over the point man and me. He must have caught at least ten rounds from the Chinese Type 53 light machine gun. It tore him in half. I dove to the ground, pulling my point man with me. How the bullets missed us I'll never know since we were directly behind him. We low crawled back into the bushes out of the clearing.

The world went crazy like it always does in a firefight. The Special Forces staff sergeant and the lieutenant spread his group and our men in a scrimmage line just outside the clearing. The lieutenant sent Sarge and our machine gunner with two men to secure the right flank. Noise from the automatic weapons and the grenades exploding was deafening, causing a ringing in my ears as the air around me filled with the smell of gunpowder. Other piles of shrubbery in the clearing became machine-gun nests. There were three of them.

After ten minutes, the shooting died down to an occasional burst, fired to keep us alert and heads down. The realization came to me that it was impossible for me to raise up enough to take the pack off my back. Someone was getting hit every minute or two. They kept us that way for an hour.

It became what combat soldiers called a "waste zone," the location where a unit got wiped out. When someone got killed, the phrase you'd hear was, "Oh, did you hear about your buddy (his name)? He got 'wasted' yesterday."

The small arms fire picked up. It looked like we were going to get wasted. Me, wasted, with my guts and body juices running out onto the ground. My eyes, blank and staring as the instant death takes hold, the moment that the soul leaves my body.

They would pick up our bodies and put them in the large green and gray casualty bags. Load us on a chopper for the ride back to base camp and graves registration. The Brothers had been right. This war was a "waste" of human life.

At first, I thought the AC-47 gunship had been a figment of my imagination. Then there it was, coming over the clearing, firing all three multi-barreled mini-guns out the left side of the plane, concentrating fire on the clearing, tearing up everything as it circled in the sky. The gunship we called "Puff the Magic Dragon" or "Spooky" made two passes, circled once more to look at the damage, then flew off.

I heard the heavy thumping sound of helicopters, a lot of them in the distance. It was the first and only time I heard anybody cheering for "The Cavalry."

The nearest reinforcements had been called in by Special Forces. Only this time, it really was the cavalry. Units of the 1st Cavalry Airmobile had been airlifted in.

Later, we found out how much we had to cheer about. We'd walked into a battalion headquarters for a North Vietnamese outfit that was training Viet Cong in the area. There had been roughly two hundred men bivouacked in the clearing, with three hundred out in the field. Recon had fewer than forty men, and there were about two dozen Montagnard with the four-man green beret's team. Nearly half were wounded or casualties by the time the cavalry rescued us. As dusk rolled around the next day, a cease-fire was called.

Memory Bank Activated: 5-2-1977
Subject: Viet Nam, 1967
Content: Telegram from the Red Cross

"Ware?"

"Yes, sir."

"Have a seat, son."

The Red Cross officer was slow in his words and actions. Before he began talking, I knew what was happening. Death had come across the water from back in the world.

We were still mopping up on the D.M.Z. operation when the vibrations came and hit me. They came strong, traveling a great distance.

Since being in Vietnam, the war had taught me the vibrations of Life, Death, Hope, Despair, and Desperation. I'd been able to sort out the incoming vibrations and classify them. Many people back in the "world," as soldiers called America, would never know that you can see death walking around like it was a real, live individual entity.

With the forecasting into the future, I'd combined the universal transcending taught to me. I knew why the Red

Cross had sent a request for me to return to field headquarters. The thought that it may be because of the Taipei incident crossed my mind. I dismissed the notion.

Vibrations had started hitting me that afternoon after the firefight when the all-clear had been called. They persisted as the choppers came in bringing hot chow, the first we'd had in a week. In the chow line, vibrations became so strong I had nearly passed out. I felt like I was dying, pain ripping my body as if hit by a full clip of rounds from a machine gun. My mess kit fell to the ground, causing everybody to turn around and look at me.

"You okay, baby brother?"

It was Davis, my homeboy from St. Louis. He and I were the only ones left from the original third squad. The rest were either dead or rotated back to the States.

"I'm okay, just tired." I bent down and picked up the mess kit. "I'm all right," I assured him.

The pain was gone. It was more mental than physical. It was a time of maximum vibrations, forcing their imprint into my being. A new experience. All the time I'd been walking through the jungle-covered mountains and valleys of the 'Nam, I'd seen lots of it, but never experienced death. Now a part of me had died in a distant place. The arrival of a supply helicopter was nothing new. The insistence of the helicopter co-pilot that I return with them had been.

On the chopper, I took the letter from my sister out of the plastic pouch and read it again. Past memories, vibrations, and the letter, all were clues that something was wrong at home. Tommy Manning's vibrations became stronger. They'd always been negative. Now they felt like the death vibrations I encountered in the chow line. I thought about making it back to the world as soon as possible. Like most Black men, I'd found that my fight wasn't in Southeast Asia. It was back on the streets where I lived and the original place of my forefather's birth.

Then the world turned upside down. Something slammed against the blades of the helicopter, stopping it in mid-flight. The chopper started spinning and spiraling down like a wounded bird with one wing. We hit the ground near the base of the hill we'd just cleared. The NVA had shot the chopper down.

The impact of the crash opened the stomach wound of the trooper the medic was transporting back to the battalion aid station. Everybody else was okay, except for minor bumps and bruises. I felt like the devil didn't want me to leave the valley of death.

Putting Satan behind me, I knew he couldn't keep me in this hell on earth. I'd been told by Master Seven that I had more important things to do than die for nothing while fighting for the wrong ideologies.

The radio wasn't damaged. The pilot had used it to call out a Mayday distress call. Twenty minutes later, a rescue chopper with an escort gunship was there to pick us up. Half an hour later, I found myself sitting in the chair, listening to what the Red Cross officer was about to say to me.

"I'm sorry, Ware. I have some bad news for you. This is a telegraph we received from the American Red Cross in Milwaukee, Wisconsin."

Holding the yellow and green piece of paper, he read very slowly, trying to give me time to get ready for what was coming. I already knew.

"There's been a death in my family?" I asked.

"I'm sorry," he said. "But there have been two deaths and an injury to another member—"

"—What!" I interrupted him…what are you saying?"

I couldn't grasp the concept; maybe I hadn't heard him right. He began reading the telegraph, skipping the formalities.

"April 22, 1967. We regret to inform P.F.C. Billy E Ware of the death of his sister, Delores, brother, Reotha and the critical wounding of his mother, Ethel. Stop. A request for P.F.C. Ware's immediate return to the States has been submitted by his family. Stop. Sincere regrets. American Red Cross, Milwaukee Chapter."

I was numb, unable to talk or move. The liaison came from behind his desk.

"Why don't you go get cleaned up and I'll have supply issue you a new travel uniform? Your company commander has been notified and has your flight orders waiting for your signature." He handed me the telegram.

"We've got a truck to take you to the airstrip. In a couple of hours, you'll be in Cam Ranh Bay catching an Air Force plane bound for the United States."

Walking out of the tent, I was still numb. I used the meditation formula to control myself, trying not to express any emotion. For I knew if I let go, I might end up going on a rampage. It was the first time I had a desire to kill someone or something.

Going into the supply tent, I walked up to Boswell, who was behind the counter."Ware, they told me to issue you new dress khakis."

He pushed the new dress uniform across the counter.

"What's happening? Where are you going?" He had noticed the strange look on my face. Finally, I found the strength to speak.

"They wasted my family," I said. "I'm going home."

"What was that?"

He didn't understand, and I didn't try to explain. Taking the bundle of clothes, I headed for the makeshift showers and the unexpected trip back to the world.

Memory Bank Activated: 5-3-1977
Subject: Back to the World
Content: War on my Home Front
My orders read: Effective 25 Apr. 1967-
casual-en route to Con U.S..

Coming back to the world was supposed to be something a vet looked forward to. I came back to the same thing I'd left in the 'Nam…death and destruction.

The funeral of my siblings became like a mirage. I walked through it in a daze. They were the closest two people to me. I began working on one thing: finding Tommy Manning.

Well aware of his activities and the places he frequented, I spent the thirty-day emergency leave making contacts. Michael was still living in Milwaukee. He was able to bring me up to date on what was happening around the city. A lot of the "Bloods" from Vietnam made it back across the water. Some of them joined the Brotherhood. Within a week, they had information for me that Tommy was hiding out on the South Side of Chicago. He'd been seen around a couple of his old hangouts. The Brothers were able to gather better intelligence than the police, who hadn't the faintest idea of his location.

If Chicago was where Tommy was, that was where I was going to be. Being a paratrooper, it was logical for me to assume they would assign me to an Airborne unit stateside. I was able to get assigned to "Casual Duty" until new reassignment orders could be cut. In order to stall for time, before my emergency leave was up, I'd gone over to Fort Sheridan and submitted a request for duty there in Illinois, knowing that the request would eventually be denied. Still, as it worked out, I was able to pull duty in the Chicago area from that May until August, and Chicago was where I wanted to be.

The Brothers were not supposed to help me locate Manning. Still, many of them volunteered their help secretly, using the cover that Manning was one of the heroin pushers they had started to investigate, trying to find ways to rid the community of them. The investigations were not made to turn the pushers over to the police, merely to observe and see how the junk was coming into the community and who was the source. Action against a pusher was only taken if the Brothers were not able to get him out of the game and we couldn't shut down his supplier.

The Brotherhood had changed. It seemed that all the guys had some type of assignment dealing with community affairs.

During the day, I was assigned light duty at Fort Sheridan. At five every evening, I'd catch the bus into Chicago, staying in an apartment on 51st and Drexel. At night, I'd walk the streets of Southside Chicago, carrying the 22-caliber pistol, the only gun I could get my hands on at the time.

Tommy had grown up in the neighborhood along the L tracks on 63rd Street and Cottage Groove Ave. Wanted for murder in Wisconsin, he'd reverted back to his old familiar hunts in Chi-town.

There were several other places I knew about. Taking them one at a time, I checked them out. After a month of duty at Sheridan, searching the streets at night for Manning and traveling to Milwaukee on the weekends, I was getting worn out. My time at Sheridan was getting short. They had little for a combat soldier to do at an administrative post. Then one hot July night, while checking out one of his old hangouts, I walked up on him!

Out of the clear blue, he came walking down the street toward me. I'd nearly called it a night, having covered a ten-block segment of the neighborhood. Turning onto 62nd

Street, I was working my way over to 63rd to catch transportation back to my apartment.

Blinking my eyes, I thought there may be a possibility that I'd been looking for him for so long that my mind was playing tricks on me. It wasn't; it was him. He was walking with his head down and his hands in his pockets. I prayed he wouldn't look up, that he would just keep walking straight toward me. The 22 cal. was in a makeshift holster strapped to my waist underneath my shirt. Pulling it out, I held it close to my leg and walked faster. I wanted to be right up on him before he could realize it.

Silently I cursed not having something larger than the 22 cal., it was a toy compared to the military weapons I was used to. I'd have to be really close to do any damage. I wanted to waste him.

There was no time to think. He was only ten feet in front of me. The alleyway was the only thing that separated us.

I pointed the pistol at his chest and shouted. "Hold it, Manning!"

He jumped back in surprise, freezing at the sight of the gun pointed at him. Slowly, he began to recognize me. It took him a few seconds because he hadn't seen me for over a year. I could read it in his face. Once he saw who it was, he knew I was going to kill him. Panicking, he turned to run. I fired.

He went down. Not from the bullet, but from a young boy who came racing down the alley riding his tricycle. Manning scrambled, trying to avoid tripping over the kid. I couldn't chance another shot, afraid I would hit the child. Tommy took off running down the alley at top speed. I took aim and squeezed the trigger. This time, nothing happened. Cursing the jammed pistol, I took out after him, trying to un-jam the revolver while on the run. I got off a second shot that missed. Manning ran onto the gangway of an apartment building.

Reaching the entrance, I stopped. It was pitch-black in the tunnel way. Having done some "Tunnel Rat" work in Vietnam, I'd learned how dangerous it was to follow blindly into a dark and unknown place. There was nothing to prevent him from hiding in the gangway and waiting for me to enter. Besides, I didn't know if he was armed or not.

Stopping, I let my eyes become accustomed to the dark, narrow enclosure. Then I slowly made my way through. A check of the gangway and back stairs of the building produced nothing. Sure that the fired shots would eventually bring the police, I gave up the search and headed back to the apartment where I was staying.

Two days later, orders came shipping me to Fort Bragg, North Carolina. The Brothers in Chicago suggested that I turn over Manning's location to the police and let them handle it. Taking their advice, I got in touch with the Milwaukee Police Department and gave them the address of Tommy's mother, who, in turn, had the Chicago Police pick up Tommy and extradite him back to Milwaukee. It had been that address I'd kept checking, knowing he wouldn't be too far away; his mother was his only family.

Having five days to make it down to North Carolina, I stopped in Milwaukee to let everybody know where I was going and to check on my mother, who had been shot by Manning during his home invasion of her house. I'd been told that Delores was staying with her and Reotha while waiting for a trial date to be set. Manning had been out on bail when the attack took place.

While I was in Milwaukee, I got a call from the police department. They were trying to verify some statements taken from Tommy, who was now being held in the County jail. In the statement, he'd said that I'd shot him.

The investigating officer asked, "Is this true, Mr. Ware?"

"No," I told him. "I haven't seen Thomas Manning. I was told by a friend in Chicago where he was hiding out, so

I called you guys to let you know. Maybe he's mad because I turned him in."

He thanked me, then hung up the phone. Leaving that day for Fort Bragg, one of the last members of my family that I saw was my niece, Angel. Tommy was her father. With Delores dead, and him doing time for that murder, I was glad that the revolver had jammed on me in Chicago. I didn't want her to grow up knowing that I caused the death of her father. These thoughts occupied my mind on the trip to North Carolina. The orders read, H. HC. 3rd BN (ABN) 325th Inf. Fort Bragg, North Carolina.

Memory Bank Activated: 5-4-1977
Subject: 1967 - On the streets
Content: Back on the streets

On the twenty-eighth of November 1967, at 7:34 A.M. after spending two-and-a-half months with the 82nd Airborne at Fort Bragg, I was officially out of the armed forces. The Brothers worked a hardship discharge for me. They had me write to Wisconsin Senator William Proxmire, explaining the deaths in my family and the need to care for my mother, who had been injured severely. The senator responded, and I got an early discharge.

My military records went from HHC 3rd BN (ABN) 325th Inf., Ft. Bragg, North Carolina to CON GP (REINF) USAAC St. Louis, Missouri, where inactive files are kept. This brought me back to the streets of Milwaukee.

It was a time of riots and protests. 'Nam vets started to change things all across the country, especially in "Brew City" Milwaukee. The people stayed uptight, and the police rode the empty curfew streets four deep in a car.

Whenever I'd meet one of the "'Nam Bloods," our conversation usually dealt with the fact that America was fast becoming what we'd left in Southeast Asia. Half of my family had died because of drugs, and not one of them had been a user of the stuff.

A lot of the Bloods smoked herbs. Mainly because that was exactly what marijuana is, an herb grown naturally, created by God, who in Holy Scriptures has told mankind to use the herbs of nature for his benefit. Vietnam had driven many a strong-minded man insane. It was not a place to live in a fog world of man-made drugs or liquor. Looking for a mild tranquilizer to use, thousands of G.I.s turned to the hemp plant.

The Brotherhood wasn't concerned about people smoking reefer. We were mainly concerned about the hard drugs that flooded the community after the riots. Knowing that the mind-altering drugs, heroin, LSD, mescaline, and the like, were being used as a control device after the riots to keep the masses and returning veterans inactive. They came from the same source that used drugs and bombs to maintain control in Southeast Asia. We knew what they were capable of, and so did the other seven million Vietnam vets. Returning veterans and the war protestors, along with the civil rights movement, were the main reasons the late sixties were so turbulent.

You can't hide from yourself. Everywhere you go, there you are. Vietnam lives in the heads of the men who served there.

I was home for about six months, working for International Harvester, and the 'Nam was still heavy on my mind. Using my G.I. home loan, I bought a house and was living with my mother, Ethel, and niece, Angel. Maintaining a day job at International Harvester, I made truck parts by day and enrolled in night school at The Career Academy School of Broadcasting, owned by a local entrepreneur named Wes Pavalon.

At the same time, I was continuing the course of study the Brotherhood had instructed me to follow, lots of history and religious studies. Word had come from Master Seven that I was to continue my assignments in the Love Section while keeping a low profile. But what I wanted really was to be in the front of the action with the marchers and demonstrators. I became heavily involved with veterans' rights and spreading the word here in the States about a little-known chemical called Agent Orange.

It had been a year and a half since I'd been contacted by the elders of the Brotherhood. They came to me on Friday, the fourteenth of February 1969. It was my birthday.

Planning on doing a little relaxing later, I headed downtown to Career Academy for my nightly classes. I'd just pulled the blue Buick Riviera I was driving to the curb on Jackson Street. It'd snowed that day, making the parking difficult. After maneuvering the car into a tight spot, I cut off the motor collected my books and got out of the car.

Still, in a state of hypervigilance, it was a habit for me to constantly be assessing my surroundings for potential threats. I spotted a man standing under a streetlight across from the school. He was dressed in a dark brown suit and overcoat with a short-brim hat. The man smiled, and I recognized him immediately. It was Morris!

Going over to meet him, we gave each other a hug and some "Dap," a special type of handshake used by Black Vietnam Vets. Then we moved into the shadows of the one-block-long city park across from the school. I took a good look at him.

"You haven't changed a bit, Brother." The fact was he was always changing.

He thanked me for doing the Taipei job when I didn't have to. I wanted to ask him about Sammy, Jomo, and Yusuf, but we both knew we couldn't share or discuss any information about other members, even among ourselves.

"Getting serious," he said. "I have a message from Master Seven. He told me to tell you that it is time for Love Section to begin its work!"

A meeting had been set for the following afternoon with a couple of the elders. For the next two years, I was once again under the tutorage of the elders of The Brotherhood of Men.

Memory Bank Activated: 5-7-1977
Subject: Turbulent Times-1969
Content: Hustling

"Well, tell me?" I asked. "How did it go?"

"No hassle, man!" he answered.

"It was the smoothest game we ever ran."

My partner, a slightly heavy-set young Brother named Hope Dye, had a satisfied look on his face as he and the lady climbed back into the car. I turned over the four fifty-five engine in the aqua blue Riviera and pulled off the lot of the appliance store, into the boulevard traffic.

Hope lit a joint and passed it to the lady in the front passenger seat. She seemed to be astonished by what she had witnessed.

"Say, that was something else," she said. "I ain't never got over on a deal like this before!" Concentrating on the traffic, I headed over to Capitol Drive, going east, back into the ghetto. The young lady started telling me what had gone down in the store.

"This salesman meets the three of us at the door see, asking us what kind of appliances we were looking for.

Sherman walked behind us not saying anything. Hope started laying a rap on this white boy about buying some furniture because we were getting married!"

Hope cuts in on the conversation.

"Yeah, and all the time I'm conning the dude, she's taking him through changes, rubbing on different parts of her body, getting him hot!"

He laughs as he passes the joint to her.

"We walked around pricing stoves and stuff so Sherman could check things out. Then he took us downstairs to look at the living room furniture."

Hope paused. He takes the joint back and takes a deep pull on the marijuana. His voice changes as he tries to hold the smoke in and keep talking at the same time.

"The young lady was wearing a short mini-skirt and a low-cut blouse. She had a body built like a 'Brickhouse' and was letting it all hang out. I could see why Hope chose her."

After exhaling from holding the smoke in his lungs, he finished the story. "By the time we got finished running game on the man, he couldn't even remember what day it was, let alone if somebody had come in the store with us!"

"Sherman disappeared so fast I didn't see him make the move."

The "Brickhouse" cutie-pie cracked up laughing.

"I saw him," she said enthusiastically, "sliding under one of the beds that had frills at the bottom!"

She let her neck go limp, resting her head on the back of the seat. The Columbian herb was taking effect. Hope taps the car seat next to her head; she looks around, and there is a folded $100 bill between his fingers. Taking the bill, she stuffs it down in her bra.

Sunset reflected from the rearview mirror let me know it was getting dark. Turning onto Hopkins Street, I pushed the Buick towards 12th Street and Fishman's place.

"Then it went okay, and everything is set?" I asked. Checking his reaction in the mirror, I could see he was pleased.

"It was really sweet, man. That was a monster idea you had, leaving Sherman behind like that." He looked at his watch. "The store should be closing at 9 P.M. We should get a call from Sherman before ten o'clock."

Making a right-hand turn on Twelfth, I drove the four blocks down to the Fishman's place, one of the popular illegal gambling spots on the Northside. They still called the slick-talking owner the Fishman, even though he'd sold his fish store years ago. His main business now was a little novelty shop with gambling in the backroom, catering to the after-hours crowd of pimps, hustlers, conmen, and streetwalkers. It was where the lady asked us to drop her off.

To her, Hope and I were just some hustlers with a slick game, big-time burglars. I'd seen her at a couple of the after-hours parties the hustler's club called "The Equals" gave in my basement sometimes. I let them use it for a share of the profits. It helped pay the mortgage on the place.

Pulling in front of Fishman's place, I stopped the car.

"It'll be three, four days before we can get you your cut of this," Hope told her. "It'll take that long to down the stuff."

She'd been a little doubtful when first hearing our plan. Now she readily agreed to anything Hope had to say.

"Okay," she answered getting out of the car. "You know where I'll be."

She gave me a sexy wink; I threw one back. Hope climbed into the front seat, slamming the door. I pulled away from the curb, going back to the house to wait for the phone call.

Back at the appliance store, there had been over two dozen TVs and component sets. We'd run the con game in order to rip the place off. Sherman and Hope were professional burglars who'd been assigned to me by the Brotherhood.

Not having a source of capital to fund the running of an organization, we were given the release to secure funds by any means necessary. The heads of the" Guerilla Section" came up with the concept of using street hustling as a blind for generating monies. They produced agents that looked, dressed, and acted like hustlers.

The "Community Control Section" figured it was an excellent way to gather information on the drug traffic that came into the North Side of Milwaukee; all kinds of documents, papers, illegal drug money, anything, and everything could be taken in a burglary without the drug dealers catching on to what we were really after. We had been instructed not to worry about marijuana dealers, who were mostly trying to make ends meet and feed their families. We were also instructed to be very selective about the places we ripped off. I hadn't told Hope or Sherman, but the places we burglarized had been chosen for political or social reasons. The "Political Section" kept us informed on the businessmen in the city who were against the social changes the Brotherhood was trying to bring about. Periodically, we were told about a store or company that wouldn't hire minorities or had unfair sales practices dealing with the minority public, but these dealing hard drugs were our main targets. They ended up on our list as the next place to hit.

We expected to make three grand from the deal going down tonight. Half went to the "Brotherhood," half to Hope, Sherman, and myself. Out of this, we'd have to drop another couple hundred on the foxy lady that helped run the game; she had two kids and no income. Hope and I went straight to the house to wait to hear from Sherman.

The call came at about 9:35 P.M., saying he had left the back door of the store open. He'd given the store owner a chance to lock up with him inside. After watching for the police to, see how they made their rounds, he went to the back door and let himself out, leaving it unlocked.

Lucky for us, the owners thought bars on the windows and double locks on the back door would be enough, so they didn't install an alarm system. Riding back to pick him up, the lessons taught to me came back to mind. In a funny way, being invisible, a "sleeper" had its disadvantages. At times, I almost forgot who and what I was. It was easy to get lost in gangster life.

Sherman stood in the shadows beside the machine shop a block from the store. As the car eased to the curb, he walked into the streetlight. Watching him approach the station wagon we used for hauling I could see the blank expression on his face. He was one of the Brothers who'd been recruited out of prison.

There was conflict within the Brotherhood on the use of gambling and selling marijuana as fundraisers. That extended to the use of people like me from Love Section as street hustlers. So guys like Sherman and Hope were recruited. The "hard time" Sherman had done was carried in the way his personality had been shaped inside the walls of the prison. It leaves some men with the need to show no emotion. Sherman was one. There was no way to read his expressionless face as he got into the car and sat down.

"The police passed the place about every two hours or so front and back," he said. "I looked at the merchandise; we'll have to make two, three hauls with this wagon."

"Come on then. Let's knock it off!" Impatience was normal with Hope. He was raring to go.

Directing my question to Sherman, I was a little more cautious. "When was the last time the squad car made its rounds?"

"Don't know for sure," he answered in his matter-of-fact manner. "They came by about fifteen minutes before I got out to call you."

Calculating the schedule of the police car and estimating how long it would take to load the wagon, I suggested that we wait until another check had been made by the police. Staying on the main boulevard, I drove up the street until we were a block from the store. Turning the station wagon around, we parked facing back down the street; this gave us a clear view of the two-lane boulevard. We sat there, watching.

A half-hour later, the squad car appeared, slowly rolling onto the parking lot of the store, shining the spotlight in the large show windows. After looking over the front, the squad car with its twin lights on top pulled around to the back, shining the searchlight on the screened windows and "supposedly" locked doors. Satisfying themselves that everything was secure, the officers continued on their rounds. We watched them moving further down the boulevard, checking the other stores.

We looked at each other. Sherman had a hint of a smile, the closest thing to an emotion I'd ever seen on his "stone face." Hope laughed out loud, slapping five with Sherman. I started the engine, and we pulled away from the curb, going to make the first of the two loads of hi-fi and TV sets.

We developed other capers, but the "Hidden Man" was one of our more successful ones. Hope and I planned and carried out eight more before we got busted.

Hope and I were hitting a sewing machine manufacturer on the South Side, just the two of us, when it happened. Sherman had been reassigned to the Detroit area two weeks earlier when his probation was up, and he could leave the state.

This hit was purely political. Research revealed that the owners of the sewing machine company were instrumental in donating large sums of money to the National Socialist (Nazi) party through a racist private club that'd also been involved in planning the mugging of a local Black civil rights spokesman who was running for public office against their candidate.

We'd trashed the private club early on a Sunday morning when no one was on the premises, painting signs that read, "compliments of the KKK: we hate Niggers & Nazis."

Maybe they would be stupid enough to start fighting each other. But apparently not. Their benefactor was smart enough to take precautions and have someone keeping an eye on his business, which was the sewing machine distribution company.

We got pulled over five blocks away from the company, having just dropped off a load of new Singer machines, still in the boxes to our fence.

Luckily, he and his partner had driven away a minute earlier. We were heading home when the police stopped us, saying that our vehicle had been spotted leaving the scene of a crime.

The problem was that there was no evidence in the vehicle. They searched the surrounding area two blocks in every direction, but could find nothing. They wanted to know what we'd done with nearly two dozen sewing machines.

I asked, "What machines?"

Hope told them he'd got a call from his girlfriend, who'd said she was at the telephone booth a few blocks down the street, asking if he could pick her up, but she was a no-show when we got there. He pointed in the direction of the sewing machine company. There was a phone booth half a block away from the place.

I could see him looking and pointing in my direction as he feed them the rest of the story.

"I asked him to drive me to pick her up because my car wasn't running," I could hear him telling the officer. They questioned us separately and got the same story. We had rehearsed it in advance.

They arrested us on suspicion anyway, believing they would eventually find or get some proof that we were the ones who committed the burglary, but they never found any; seems the alarm system with its videotape camera wasn't working for some unknown reason.

After spending two weeks in the county jail, I received an arraignment. Bail was set, and a trial date was given. I got word to the fence that had been handling the merchandise for us and he had an associate of his post bail for us. I was back on the streets.

During the time spent in the county jail, I read, studied, and learned quite a bit about the criminal justice system. I hadn't liked the life of a street hustler, but at the time, it was the only way for me to keep from going under financially.

After coming home from Vietnam, I had a lot of trouble with my respiratory system. From 1968 until the present, several times a year, every year, I've been diagnosed and hospitalized with cases of pneumonia, bronchitis, chronic sinusitis, and calcified nodules in the left lung. You can't work a job if you are laid up with these ailments for weeks at a time every two or three months out of the year. The V.A. said they didn't know what the cause was. I think it's from Agent Orange. But in the 1970s, there were no benefits from exposure to the chemicals. As the Vietnamese say, *Xin Loi vi Dieu do* (Meaning: Sorry about that).

Memory Bank Activated: 5-13-1977
Subject: Higher Knowledge 1971
Content: Changing Times

"It's simple," Morris was telling me. "Use the education benefits from your military service to finance the classes, you've still got a lot of eligibility." He was answering the question I'd asked him in regard to my new assignment, which was in colleges, and universities, the higher education institutions.

When the legal repercussions came down from the burglary, the elders used the excuse to snatch me off special duty with the hustlers. The court gave me a public defender and said there was no need for a trial. The public defender told the court I have no prior record, I was not found with any of the stolen merchandise in my possession, and I was a combat veteran who had serviced his country honorably.

Since I had no priors and there was no proof, he thought that my being a military veteran should allow him to be lenient and only sentence me to a year of probation with supervision. Hope got six months in the house of corrections because he was a felon out after curfew and "may have" been part of a crime.

Memory Bank Activated: 5-14-1977
Subject: Higher Knowledge 1971
Content: Changing Times

Morris and I were down in the basement of the house I'd bought on 25th and Keefe Avenue. The Brotherhood was using it now as a "safe house" for members moving cross-country. To get a definite view of what was happening with the "nightlife" side of each city, a program was instituted sending Brothers to hang out in the local taverns. Liquor loosens lips.

Still fighting to clean up the hard drugs coming into the community, a lot of information was gathered and then channeled back to the Community Control Section, and if necessary, a team was put into action. Morris was handling the mechanics of the operation on a national scale. He was in Milwaukee for a briefing on the set-up here. I invited him to stay at my house. It was after we'd made the rounds and gone back to the house that Morris told me what the elders were planning for me. It was the last of March 1971.

Bunking out on the couch in the basement, Morris straightened out his arms and yawned. "You got to come out of that hustling bag and concentrate on this new assignment. A lot of things are happening politically, socially, and in every other way. We're going to need young brothers that have their heads together, and with a good education, This temporary job you've got at the Boy's Club will keep the man off your back and give you an opportunity to help a lot of young people stay on the right path."

Stretching out on the couch, he closed his eyes, unable to fight the beckoning darkness that flooded his mind. He hadn't slept at all during the past two days.

I sat in the stuffed chair, listening to the soft jazz from the John Coltrane album, watching him, thinking about what we'd been through together. It didn't seem real.

By June, when the summer session started, I was to be enrolled at Milwaukee Area Technical College, majoring in general education with an emphasis on communication skills.

Since the "sewing machine" incident, the elders had one of the Brothers find a part-time job for me with the Lavarnway Unit of the Milwaukee Boy's Clubs, Inc. This had been arranged by the organization in order to give me the appearance of a rehabilitated felon who'd seen the light and gone straight.

Personally, I enjoyed working with the kids, being an all-around handyman and part-time counselor. My job was really nondescript.

Most of my time was spent in the one-room branch library on the second floor reading the vast array of books on Black history. It was there that I gained an in-depth insight into who I was as a Black man in America and who my ancestors had been as Black men in Africa. During seven months of working at the center, I read the complete volume of Black history books and a number of novels in the media and entertainment fields.

Vibrations told me the literature on the shelves was planned, designed especially for me to further my knowledge on particular subjects. Vibrations proved me right again when, after a week, a new man was hired to work with me. He was a young brother of the Muslim faith. It became obvious why he was there: to teach me about Islamic beliefs. I was eager to learn.

History was my favorite subject in school. You cannot study world history without studying the different religions. History is made up of religions, and these different beliefs have caused more conflicts than anything else between human beings. Although I hadn't adopted any one particular faith at that time, I opened my mind to absorb the wisdom of the teachings, just as I had from the Christian ministers I'd encountered in my youth. I found the 114 Surahs in the Holy Quran to be of the highest order and adopted as many of the customs as possible, while still keeping my cover. One thing I'd learned was that it all seemed to point in one direction. Muhammad was confirming the teaching of the Prophets Abraham, Jesus, Buddha, and Confucius. Like the qualities a Hindu must have to be a "Brahmin," all have the ability to forgive, follow truth, avoid sinful activities and to be a seeker of knowledge and educate others.

I began to see how these things related to me, a poor Black man in the slums of North America. My mission was becoming clearer. Was I really who the Brothers said I was?

For periods of a year or more, events in my existence were normal, as a matter of fact, boring. Then suddenly, Morris would show up and tell me my life was due for another drastic change.

Yet, it wasn't only me, the whole world was changing. I could feel the vibrations when I looked at the protestors demonstrating against the war in Vietnam or listen to the people complaining about getting screwed by the man in the White House they called "Tricky Dicky."

Little did the people know that five years later, on August 8, 1974, President Richard Nixon would resign from office because of a scandal called Watergate.

How did this happen? On June 17, 1972, at 1 A.M., a young Black Brother named Frank Wills, who was the security guard working for $80 bucks a week at the Watergate complex in Washington, DC, would call the police to report a break-in at the office of the Democratic National Committee inside the complex. The break-in would be traced all the way back to the White House and President Richard Nixon.

Yes, change was coming to America and the whole world. Thinking of this change brought a smile to my face. I sat in the chair and nodded off to sleep.

Memory Bank Activated: 5-17-1977
Subject: Higher Knowledge 1971
Content: Power in the Word

"Automatic, Pushbutton-Remote Control, Synthetic Genetics. Control your soul!"

The young white college students sat spell bond, not believing what they were hearing from the three Black students in their oral interpretation class. Chanting the lyrics, Roy Ogletree, Floyd Debow, and I did the choreography we'd worked out a week earlier.

The poetry of the Last Poets, a popular recording group among young Black activists, was powerful and provocative. We'd chosen the group for its strong anti-establishment message. The middle and upper-class white kids had never heard Black people reciting poetry with stanzas and verses like "THE WHITE MAN'S GOT A GOD COMPLEX!" pointing the finger at them, telling them about their forefather's racist past and their doomed future if they don't change the social and political system.

The assignment was for the oral interpretation class at Milwaukee Area Technical College. It was the beginning of my second semester at school.

I'd missed the first week of class, having a task to perform for the elders. Upon returning to school that Monday, I was putting my things away in my hall locker when Roy, whom I called Tree, walked up.

"Say, stranger, where you been?" He was probing again.

"With a sick relative," I told him.

Putting my coat in the locker, we headed for the morning class.

"We still got time to get with Floyd and practice before Professor Riley's oral interpretation class this afternoon," I volunteered. I'd been doing that ever since the day he talked to me about doing some kind of entertainment project together. He'd come all the way from LaGrange, Georgia, to attend the local community college here in Milwaukee. Vibrations made me suspect he had more than a scholarly interest in being here in Brew City and in me.

It was the two words I wasn't supposed to hear when I'd agreed to work with him on the joint school project. He hadn't intended for me to hear them, or for them to have any meaning, but they had. To me, they held great meaning. I wasn't supposed to hear him as he turned and walked away.

"Got you," was all he said.

The vibrations hit me like a giant wall of seawater, and I went under, the alarm bells ringing in my head, warning me. A mental picture of Tree's face was grinning at me from above the water's surface. I felt a sharp pain in my lower lip, like I'd just bitten down on a hook. I was being pulled out of the water toward Tree's face; he was looking at me like I was a fish he'd hooked. His mental image grinned, then vanished.

"Got you."

Thinking about our first meeting, I suppressed the smile that longed to come to my face as we walked to class. Who was fooling who? I didn't want him to know that this time the fisherman had caught a killer whale.

Just before going into the classroom to give the oral presentation, Tree told me that he was preparing to transfer to the University of Wisconsin-Milwaukee, and he could get me in on the same program if I wanted to make the switch.

Tree was being helpful, in a way, too helpful…he introduced me to girls, came up with spending money, and also introduced me to influential people on a local and national scale. This aroused my suspicions. He was doing all this for a reason.

After a while, people at the school started to notice that I was a loner and didn't belong to any of the cliques at the school. Being an individualist is one way of shining the spotlight on yourself. I didn't have to wait long before everybody was interested in finding out, as the saying goes, "where my head was at." The professor asked that very question at the end of our three-man performance of the Last Poets in his class.

"That was different! I don't think we have experienced anything quite like this in class before. What were you thinking Billy, when you chose this particular piece; what was your reason? Where was your head at?"

"Love and understanding, that's where my head is at," was my answer.

Floyd and Tree looked at me. The statement was impromptu.

Walking back to my seat, I watched as the other aspiring communicators gave their performances. I could see Tree was happy. He knew what we had just done gave us an *A* out of the class. Tapping him on the shoulder, I whispered in his ear, "That University of Wisconsin thing; count me in!"

The next semester, I was at the University of Wisconsin-Milwaukee.

Memory Bank Activated: 5-21-1977
Subject: Higher Knowledge 1972
Content: Campus Life

UWM. wasn't the only thing Ogletree got me into. He introduced me to a young lady by the name of Diana Mudd, who, in turn, was instrumental in getting me involved with a local veteran's organization, which, at the time, was called Interested Veterans of the Central City. Although Diana was the one who informed me of the meetings being held by the group, I could feel the hand of Ogletree controlling the strings that made the puppets move. Since I was a Vietnam Vet, the idea of joining a veterans' group didn't seem unusual. What was unusual was the fact that Ogletree was not a veteran, but was always wanting to tag along when I went to meetings. Like a fisherman reeling in a fighting Marlin, you let him run for a while before you reel in the line.

Besides getting me involved with the I.V.O.C.C. veterans' organization, he secured part-time jobs for me at local radio and television stations. After a short period of time, it became obvious to me that I was fast becoming a part of some sort of "mass conspiracy." This became even more obvious when Tree started steering me in the direction of the Omega Psi Phi fraternity, along with several young musicians that also attended U.W.M.

The fall semester of 1973 began. Tree had spent the summer, it seems, paving the way for me to meet certain people, among them Horace Parks, who was a Mason, member of Omega, and a media salesman for the WNOV radio station located in Milwaukee.

At the time, I was still working part time as a floor director at a local television station while attending school. Roy came up with the idea of starting the first Omega chapter on the U.W.M. campus, and supposedly Horace Parks was the link between the graduate chapter of the fraternity and our group of potential student pledges. I'd gone along with the plans, keeping my suspicions to myself. It was one cool fall night when it became clear what they were trying to get me involved in.

Tree and I were returning from the evening class we had. Coming into Sandburg dorms, where we roomed, we ran into another student whom Tree was trying to get to pledge the fraternity. His name was Ben Evans, and he was a talented musician, a flutist, also enrolled at the Wisconsin Conservatory of Music. Roy was quick to point this out also that Ben was a vet who'd spent his time overseas in Europe. I was surprised that Roy knew Ben. This heightened my suspicions. Roy had never been in the service, and he was of an opinion that all vets were alike. I found it impossible to explain to him that non-combat vets and combat veterans were as different as peas and carrots. The ideologies and experiences were different.

Roy insisted that we follow Ben up to the suite of rooms he occupied with several other musician students. Taking the elevator to the top floor of the south tower of the dorm complex, we got off and entered the suite. The place was crowded. Amplifiers and microphones were set up, and three other musicians were there along with a couple of groupies.

Ben introduced us to the boys in the band, Don Cole, who played lead guitar, a bass guitarist named Cid Duncan, and a young drummer they called Poncho. They were sitting around, tuning up their instruments. One of the groupies that hung out with the band began to fool around with the mic, trying to do one of the old standards that the musicians were working on. Everybody got on her case because of her inability to carry the tune.

One by one, everyone was encouraged to give it a go at the mic. I stayed out of it, watching them. After everyone in the room had taken a turn, Tree looked at me.

"Why don't you give it a try?"

I played the shy role, smiling and shaking my head. "Not me, man," I told him. "I haven't done any singing for a long time."

Deep inside, I longed to work with the mic. I'd always felt a great love for music, any kind of music. They wouldn't take no for an answer. After a fair amount of coaxing, I agreed. We worked on some of the old "do-wops" from the fifties and sixties. By the end of the night, everybody was convinced that we should start meeting after classes on a regular basis.

At first, I'd backed out, saying I didn't want to get involved because I had very little musical training and my respiratory system was shot to hell. But they wouldn't let it slide. From then on, every afternoon after class, Tree and I would eventually end up on the twentieth floor of the south tower working with the group.

Knowing there was an ulterior motive for Ben and the group devoting so much time to an untrained person like myself, I began to watch the situation very closely. Within a week or so, all kinds of people and drugs began to show up at the rehearsal sessions.

The group was joined by a white guitarist by the name of Bill Hogan, and a lovely young Black songstress named

Debbie Williams. There was always a large amount of cocaine and marijuana that just "happened" to be on the scene.

Cocaine is an expensive drug and not something that people give away (in quantity), not unless they have a reason. I found out what they had in mind one Friday night we'd gotten together for a session. That night, the drugs and wine were especially plentiful, and everybody at the session was pretty high. I'd consumed a moderate amount of the wine and felt the effects of breathing in secondhand smoke from the marijuana, giving the impression that I was just as high off the combination of secondhand smoke and wine as everybody else was of the harder drugs.

Once the session was going full blast, Tree came up with the idea of doing impromptu numbers off the top of our heads. People started competing in front of the mic. As usual, I hung in the background as much as possible, standing upside the wall, watching the others.

Slowly, I began to feel a stronger reaction than seemed normal for the amount of stimulus I'd taken into my system. Remembering my training, I realized that I'd been slipped some kind of drug other than what I'd taken. From my body's reactions, it felt like some type of stimulant. Speed maybe… put in the wine? Speed (amphetamine) lowers inhibitions and tends to make a person extremely talkative. At the time, I didn't know it, but that was what they wanted from me, to be more talkative, much more.

Listening to the musicians working on an unnamed tune, I searched for the reason for the possible drugging, knowing it had something to do with the music. From my research, I knew that drugs were used in the music and entertainment industry to control artists and keep them in a state of dependency. They were a major part of the game that had been run on great artists like Billie Holiday and others who'd been misused and abused by the money people of the music industry. Now they were thinking it was my turn. The con game became perfectly clear. They were going to try to pick my brain with drugs, women, and good times. They were going to try to drain me of all the intellectual property they could get.

My mind sought a solution. Should I play along with them, or should I bust the con game wide open? The drugs rushed through my body, boggling my mind and heightening my emotions to the point of exploding. They were pushing me to let the angry, pinned-up feelings run free. Fighting the effects of the drugs and the music, I left the suite and went down to my room on the third floor. I had to think the situation out without the drugs in my system.

Memory Bank Activated: 5-17-1977
Subject: The Love Music, 1973-74
Content: Con for the Conman

"Well, what are you going to do?"

Morris sat in the large stuffed red chair on the other side of the basement. It'd taken three days to get in touch with him. During that, I avoided Roy and Ben, claiming to have a busy schedule and other interests besides the music. There were many factors I had to consider relating to how they were planning to use me. I knew that what was happening was standard industrial practices in the entertainment field for the stealing of intellectual property. I had to find out from the Brotherhood what they felt about the situation.

Morris came with a warning. The elders had checked out the information I'd provided on the suspected con game. I was unprepared for the data they had entrusted to Morris. It seemed as if things were slightly more complicated than I'd imagined.

The organizations and people that Roy had gotten me involved with had connecting links with just about every political, social, and religious entity in the country. Most were Black organizations with European ideologies, such as Greek-letter fraternities. Another, the Free Masons was international in its scope.

Morris summarized the file he held in his lap. "From what the Brothers have been able to gather in the way of information on why you've been chosen, and the way they've collectively banded together is clear to the elders; the different groups that are a part of this 'mass conspiracy' recognized your profit-making potential and have become interested in capitalizing on you. The utilization of individuals for personal profit is at the heart of the American economic system, always has been."

"I think it's that damn Aquarian personality of yours," he said half in jest. "You're too much of a humanitarian, Brother."

Then he became serious. "These people want to use you, Billy, all the time hoping you will become a dope addict or sex freak so they can control you with drugs or some big-assed woman. And they do it all with computers."

"Computers?" I rose from the couch, not sure what he meant.

"Yeah, it's a hell of a system they have, recording you without your knowing it. Once they plug the new, original lyrics you've just created into the computer, the songs are broken down into types, then issued to different artists via songwriters already associated with the artist and who are well known in the industry. Since the material they take is usually from some poor Black person who has no idea of what an elaborate trap he or she has fallen into, they usually end up with the copyrights, distribution, and sales rights to the songs they steal."

"You're not the first person out of the ghetto that they've run this game on. Seems like this is the norm in the music industry. Most people wouldn't be able to figure out what was happening to them until it was too late, but you did."

He smiled. "That was one reason why you were given the type of training you received."

I leaned back on the arm of the couch, staring at the basement ceiling. "How does my training come into play on this particular setup?" I asked.

Looking for a solution to the dilemma, Morris put his elbows on the arms of the chair, interlacing his fingers together. He sat there silently, watching me.

He spoke slowly. "When the Watergate incident happened, it changed the entire spectrum of political affairs in this country. Eventually, it will have a profound effect on the entire world. This earth-shattering event came about because of the Brother Frank Willis, who was a security guard at the Watergate complex. A cover-up has been in operation since the break-in, and these very same people who control the government control the outflow of media information; and as you know, the media controls the minds of most Americans."

"That's one reason for your training, to infiltrate you into the media industry so we could develop a counter-brainwashing entity. To get rid of the idea that people in power are supermen, cause we know ain't no such thing as a superman."

"Brothers from Love Section have been planted in every major faction of this society, religion, politics, business, education, and other fields, such as yourself, in communications. You, as a sleeper, have been undergoing specialized training for the last fourteen years! The elders feel it is time for the sleepers to wake up! You can be a catalyst for change. The organizations and people behind this thing you've gotten yourself into are supposed to live by the oaths they have taken. Oaths like believing in a Supreme Being, Brotherly Love, relief from injustice, and Truth. They say they want to uplift you, help you build your manhood through Perseverance and Scholarship."

"Okay," I told him. "Let's put them to the test. If I let them take the intellectual property God has granted me, and me alone, what will they do with it?"

Morris was thinking too. "Are they doing it just to rip you off and profit themselves, or is it to uplift you as one of their brothers? Will you share in the profits? Get a slice of the money cake they want you to bake?"

I jumped in. "Or is it to gobble up the whole cake, gobble, gobble, and leave me to starve?"

"They won't let you create anything for yourself." Morris continued, "If you don't work for them, then you don't get to work at all in the business."

We'd seen both sides of these fraternal private clubs. Some say that they are good for our people, and some say they are tools of the establishment, gatekeepers allowed to exist to keep the rest of us from advancing.

Then he began to fill me in on the long-range political, economic, and social goals of the worldwide counsel for The Brotherhood of Men.

There were two priorities on top of the list concerning the communications industry. One was making minorities as a group and the country as a whole aware of the current political situation and preparing them to withstand the vast amount of propaganda and misinformation that the Nixon administration would be leaking to the press, trying to play down the seriousness of the burglaries that had taken place at Watergate.

The other was making Black people, in particular, aware of themselves and their heritage, while providing economic platforms for them that are independent and solely controlled by them.

Love Section was designed to bring about a new awareness, thereby making the atmosphere more conducive, enabling the message that was carried by the Brotherhood to be delivered to the world.

While he was talking, a bizarre, weird plan began to develop in my head. Vibrations bombarded my brain. I felt high and elated, like I normally did when a new concept began to formulate in my mind.

The idea was so inspiring to me it sprung me up from the couch, roaring in laughter. Morris sat there with a puzzled look on his face.

"You think this is funny, Billy?" He was getting angry. "The things we'd been discussing are extremely serious!"

"I'm sorry," I apologized. "But I think I may have found a solution that will solve both the Brotherhood's problem of getting the message out from the Love Section to the people *and* my situation with the music at the university, all at the same time!"

"Don't hand me that crap." Morris had no idea what I was talking about. "In order to pull something like this off, we'd have to have a hell of a propaganda machine! We don't have enough Black-owned radio and TV facilities to mass distribute our philosophies. And you tell me you've got the solution to all our problems!"

The idea was so simple that at first, I thought he may be right. Then I realized it was not a spur-of-the-moment conception, but the end result of fourteen years of study, meditation, and just maybe a gift of God-given inspiration.

"Let me see the data we have on the network they use for distribution of the lyrics they've taken so far," I asked.

"What good will that do?" he wanted to know.

I calmed him down. "Relax. If I am who the Brothers say I am, then it will be done, right?"

He looked into my eyes and could see that I was sincere about what I was saying. Slumping back in his seat, a smile crossed the corners of his mouth. He handed me the green data sheets on the operation we had named "Mass Conspiracy."

"Anyway, now is the time for action," he said. "If you've got an idea, let's hear it, and I'll take it back to the elders."

Listening, I told him what my idea was, and slowly, he began to understand where I was coming from.

"Maybe you are who they say you are." He chuckled.

"I'll need a day or two to make sure my concepts are sound, and there's one thing you can do for me," I asked.

"What's that?" he wanted to know.

"If the idea is sound, I'll need permission to totally open up, declare who I am."

Morris sat in silence. He knew that exposing myself and who I was to the powers controlling America could very well cost me my life.

Memory Bank Activated: 5-21-1977
Subject: 1974-Love Music
Content: Message Music

Putting everything together started with a trip to the Brotherhood Political Section for the Midwest area, temporarily located in Chicago. There I could get a forecast of the Brotherhood's expected agenda of events up until the year 1980. All the headquarters groups for the Brotherhood were kept on a mobile basis, traveling around the country, sometimes even across the borders. For once, they all met in the same location, Chicago.

I was supposed to be standing on the sidelines, waiting to talk to the elders while the executive types concluded their meeting. Love Section was still a thing of the future for most of the members; it didn't work out that way. My activities became the topic of the day once they found out what kind of information I had gathered and what my plan entailed.

The conference was being conducted in a downtown office building. The Brothers had simply put on their suits and ties, donned a briefcase, and played the businessman's con game, mingling with the standard nine to fivers who crowded the downtown loop of Chicago, filtering up to the top floor of the swank building.

I was one of the last to arrive. Getting off the elevator and walking down the hall, I heard part of a conversation coming out of the meeting room.

First voice: "What's Dr. Strangelove talking about doing now?"

Second voice: "I don't know… Doesn't look like he does much of anything if you ask me."

First voice: "Know what you mean! I thought he was some kind of pimp or hustler when I first met him!"

Second voice: "Yeah, especially when they said he was in charge of the 'Love Section.'" Laughter erupts in the room.

Dr. Strangelove, so that was the nicknames the Brothers had given me. Making jokes about my being a mad scientist, walking around babbling about changing the world with formulas that no one understood.

What I heard brought a smile to my face. The more unbelievable I was to people, the better I felt, seeing that my mission was to bring about truth from the unbelievable.

Opening the door, I stepped into the boardroom and immediately I knew there was going to be opposition to my idea. I could see and feel it as I looked around the table.

I was considered a joke! The funny little man who sat around staring off into space. I knew some of them felt I had a severe case of PTSD and needed counseling.

Meditation and awareness training had taught me to overcome ridicule and pressure from outside sources. I used calming techniques to prepare for the argument that was coming. The more relaxed I became, the better my chances of winning my case.

A Brother by the name of Robert was the chief of the Political Section. He opened it up for questioning, then each section head had his turn digging into me. They were mostly concerned about the effects on society of the psychological stimulus injected through the mass communications networks that the music industry was a part of. That included records sales, radio play, TV music videos, and even soundtracks for movies.

The Community Control Section head was the most opposed to the plan. He wanted data so they'd be able to take the data and make an accurate forecast for three to five years in the future on the possible effects of the stimuli.

I keep insisting that it was normal for material things like urban cities and populations to be pre-planned years in advance, but impossible for someone to be able to foresee exactly what the political, social, and economic outcome would be for the next five years from the injection of a mood-altering suggestive stimuli into a world's mass populous.

The argument became so intense, a vote was called. It ended in a deadlock. Because of the short time limit in reaching a decision, a call was put into Master Seven. His vote would break the tie.

After Robert talked to him for a couple of minutes, he waved me over. "He wants to talk to you," he said.

I walked around the table and took the phone from him, putting it to my ear. "Yes, sir."

For some reason, I still pictured him as the tall young man I'd met years earlier. I hadn't spoken to him personally since then; his voice brought the memories flooding back.

"Billy, Morris filled me in on what you have in mind. It's not the way we expected things to happen. I guess everybody's uptight about that."

"Do you think doing this will help us reach our goals?"

"Yes, I do!" I said it with as much conviction as I could muster.

He sounded like he might go along with me. I pressed on.

"From what I've been able to assess, it's time for me to activate my section, sir. With the so-called 'hippies' and their countercultural movement promoting a lifestyle of love and peace, there is no better time. Music is a catalyst that will not only reach the people here in America, but the entire world."

He paused for a moment, then very slowly he said, "You might be right. I just hope your timing isn't off and you're left hanging out on a limb…one that's being sawed off. You understand that if anything goes wrong, there isn't much we can do for you! You'll be entirely on your own?"

"I understand that, yes, sir," I told him, glad I'd won him over.

"Let me speak to Robert, and good luck, my Brother!"

I handed the phone back to the Political Section chief. He spoke to Master Seven, nodding his head in agreement while getting the master's instructions, then he hung up the phone. Everybody around the table had their eyes glued to him, waiting to hear how the master had voted.

Robert eased it out. "He says to let him go ahead."

The meeting adjourned, and I drove back to Milwaukee. Three days later, I was back on the twentieth floor of Sandburg Towers at U.W.M. hanging out with the boys in the band.

After a brief period of the nightly sessions, I started having problems with my singing voice. The respiratory problems from Vietnam continued to make holding notes and breathing difficult. I suggested to Tree that we try something a little different.

"Why don't we use a style similar to what we did with the poetry back at MATC, but more musical, you know, kind of rapping the lyrics instead of singing them?" I'd done a few original tunes like that in earlier sessions.

That night, I began to work on the innovative approach in earnest. Ogletree had gotten to the point of laying in the background and making suggestions for various kinds of song lyrics. He started talking about television cowboy shows, and as usual, I was supposed to express my opinion. The old, how would you tell this story game, which is a fantastic way to extract intellectual concepts from an unsuspecting person under the influence of drugs. I acted like a hooked fish willing to take the bait, hook, line, and sinker.

Tree asked, "What kind of cowboy movie would you make if you were writing one?"

This was my opportunity. I jumped at the chance. "Who, me? I'd do a story they've never seen before… I'd shoot the sheriff."

Everybody broke up laughing, thinking I was making a joke; I wasn't. I was thinking of the movement to impeach

Nixon (whom I thought of as the crooked sheriff) and get rid of his (deputies) Mitchell, Haldeman, Ehrlichman, Hunt, Liddy, and a host of others.

I pushed the idea. "Let me tell you what I'm talking about."

The lyrics poured out like a western ballot. Forming the concept in my mind, I stepped up to the microphone. Ben and the rest of the group began playing, and I began adding the "impromptu" lyrics to the instrumental. The song began to flow from my lips, without a pause or a word being written down. In the end, I shoot the sheriff, but the people of America shoot the deputies. In all, a total of forty government officials got caught up in the scandal.

After the piece was completed and the musicians stopped playing, everybody was noticeably quiet. Tree leaned against the window with a satisfied smile on his face. They had expected to get something out of me, but not all this! The lyrics told of a conflict between a farmer and the local sheriff in a western town, but you could feel that it was an analogy of the current political situation happening in the capital. All of "Tricky Dicky's" underlings, his "deputies" so to speak, were getting wasted politically.

Memory Bank Activated: 5-23-1977
Subject: 1973-74, U.W.M.
Content: The Love Music

There were at least a dozen people lining the walls of the dorm room. The rehearsal sessions had become a circus. We'd been at it from the middle of the fall semester of '73 to the spring of '74. It'd gotten to the point where they started to bring different people in to watch us create the new music.

My reputation for being aloof from the crowd had begun to grow. Inwardly, my main concern was controlling the wording of each consecutive tune, making sure that a small portion of the love formulas was woven into the lyrics of each new song. I then made sure that the following one had the next sequence. By doing this, I was creating a psychological stimulus in the mind of the listener. Hearing two or three of these "love songs" a day, it would induce a change in an individual's thinking pattern. To make sure what I was doing wasn't detected too early, I'd only do soft "love" type numbers when anyone but a few friends and the boys in the band were around, saving the hard-hitting political concepts for more private sessions.

The semester was ending, and I was pushing the music. Sometimes keeping the group up until the wee hours, doing three or four original tunes a night. Not knowing how long they would keep up the con, I wanted to get in as much material as possible.

After doing the music, I would go back to my room and try to get some rest. Because of the night sessions with the music, I'd shifted my reading and studying to early mornings and afternoon hours. My classes were coming to an end, and so was the music.

The band had decided it was time to see how we would be received by an audience, so Ben booked us in a couple of local nightclubs for one-night stands. I was glad people would see us out in public.

With about a week left, everyone was beginning to pack up the dorms. I began to think maybe these guys were on the level, and maybe we could pick up the pieces and they would do the brotherly thing and cut me off a slice of the cake I'd baked for them. Anyway, it was time for me to confront them and find out. If anyone needed to be uplifted and shown some "Brotherly Love" it was me, a poor Black man who had given them everything. Was I to be left with nothing?

Memory Bank Activated: 5-25-1977
Subject: 1974-1977
Content: Aftereffects

That summer, the songs began to hit the charts. Slowly at first, then the number increased with alarming speed. Ben had taken an apartment on the east side of town. I spent the majority of my time at his place, practicing on a bass clarinet, which held a strange attraction for me. Ben was supposed to be teaching me to read music, but from his attitude, I was able to tell that he resented me for some reason. I found out what was on his mind the day I confronted him about the songs ending up on the commercial charts. The new genre we'd created would go on to produce thousands of jobs and rake in billions of dollars in record sales for people who would normally never have been able to enter the industry.

At first, he refused to acknowledge the fact that anything at all had happened.

Finally, under my repeated questioning about how and why the music we created ended up being recorded by a bunch of other people, he said, "Well, you shouldn't get involved in things you don't know anything about."

Asking me to leave the apartment, he turned and walked away. From his mannerisms, I wondered if he was jealous of the lyrics that were becoming so popular.

Then it hit me; with the nature of the "Mass Conspiracy," none of these extremely talented musicians would be able to lay claim to the music we'd made. They were in the same boat as I was on that score. Would they be getting some kind of financial benefits? That I did not know.

How would Leonardo da Vinci have felt if he heard and saw someone else being praised every time a person looked at his painting of the *Mona Lisa* and his mural of *The Last Supper*?

As an artist, I felt sorry for him. He was still unaware of the nature of the songs and what their intended purpose was. At least I had that. Still, it would have been good to have a piece of the pie; being poor in America and watching other people grow rich and famous from your intellectual property can produce a lot of hate in your heart if you are not strong in fate in God and the purpose he has put you here for.

I decided it was time to cut ties with members of the band. They had begun to avoid me anyway, confirming that the "Mass Conspiracy" had been a rip-off scheme from the beginning.

Around that same time, the tunes that made the airwaves in the summer of 1974 were mostly love ballads or soft jazz pieces. They seemed harmless and yet slightly different from standard R & B pieces, a blend of disco and jazz.

I took the job that Horace Parks offered me, working with Vernon Wilkerson, who was the sales manager at WNOV radio station as a salesman, creating the thirty- and sixty-second commercial spots needed for the airtime sold by the station.

Ogletree and I were still on friendly terms; even with the possibility of him being the front man for the Mass Conspiracy; at least we were until I confronted him about the music we'd created being done by well-known artists. He didn't want to talk about it at first. Then he'd made a reference to Ben Evans being the one who ripped me off. My belief was that they were all trying to cover their own asses. The mark is not supposed to know they are being conned and confront the conman.

Late that summer, the songs hit the radio airwaves with increased force. The unusual lyrics caught everyone's ear. Instead of one or two of the tunes being played, whole albums of the music came on the market. Then slowly, piece by piece, the message music began to appear on the scene.

Listening to the radio and hearing the lyrics, I knew that my plan was working. They hadn't cut out any of the songs. Like I figured, they had taken them in wholesale. There were a lot of artists and groups that were "Bustin Out" of their L seven squares. I even had the white boys playing that funky music.

The unknown and seldom seen power brokers of the music industry, the people involved in the Mass Conspiracy, started coming to Milwaukee to take a look at me. They wanted more content, and for the same price, for nothing.

Along with all this came the pimps, hustlers, and con artists, trying to get more material out of me by setting me up with a lady, or becoming my friend who would steer me onto drugs and into the trap of the rip-off artist. It didn't work.

The music I'd done at U.W.M. was the only material they would get from me, unless I was employed to produce lyrics by someone who was willing to pay. Even though the "Love Music" wasn't intended to be a profit-making venture, it was, extremely so. And to this day, not one of those who made their fortune from the music has offered to help me in any way. I have not seen one thin dime from the billions made from the sales of the music.

By the fall of 1974, Ogletree had gone back south to Georgia. He'd graduated that spring semester, and although he stated that he was staying around Milwaukee to work with me, his ulterior motive was to "milk the cow dry." While they were trying to milk the cow, the cow was taking over the dairy farm.

The music became more political in nature. With the populace of the country listening to anti-propaganda music all day, it was becoming more and more difficult for the Nixon administration to convince the people of their good nature and intentions. Every time they'd tell the lie that they were the good guys like superman, one of the songs would hit the streets letting the people know that there "Ain't No Such Thing as A Superman" and the truth will always come to light.

With mass support from the common people, the government began to prosecute members of the Nixon administration, and finally, "Tricky Dicky" Nixon was forced to resign. The automatic brainwashing machine that was used on most Americans had been broken by a message in the music and general awareness of the people. They were telling Richard Nixon that despite all he claimed to have done for this country, in reality, "You Haven't Done Nothin'."

Memory Bank Activated: 5-27-1977
Subject: Necromancers (talk show)
Channel 10-Milwaukee, Wisconsin
Content: Topic of the show for 3-22-77
"Is There Too Much Sex in the Music?"
Participants of the show are: Talk Show
Host Carol Malone
Guests: 0. C. White- WAWA Radio
Personality.
Mannie Mauldin-Syndicated Jazz Show Host
Larry "the legend" Johnson - WZUU Radio
J. Johnson - Disc Jockey WNOV Radio
Rev. George Reddick, Operation Push,
Chicago, Ill.

A studio audience numbering two dozen people, including myself, is in attendance. At approximately 9:05 P.M., after thirty minutes of opinions expressed by the guest panel and telephone calls from the home audience, the host Carol Malone opens up the show to questions from the studio audience. I get to ask the third question.

"Good evening. My name is Billy E. Ware. I'd like to know if any of you have information concerning the belief that eighty percent of this 'sex music' or 'love music' that has been produced for the last three years in the record industry comes from a small group of individuals that attended the University of Wisconsin-Milwaukee during the 1973-74 semester. And there is a novel being written about the incident and the exploitation of the creators of this music?"

After several seconds of silence, the radio announcer, O. C. White, answers, "No, we don't think there is a conspiracy behind the music."

Wondering why he used the term "conspiracy," I start to give some details and facts to back up my statement, but I'm cut off by the host who asks Rev. George Reddick of Operation Push his opinion of my statement. He agrees with O.C. White and reaffirms what the panel of guests has been saying, that the music is corrupting the populist by telling them to "Do it!... Do it til your satisfied, whatever it is!" And things like the seeking of "Sexual Healing."

I try to get the host's attention, but I am ignored. Time runs out. At 9:29 P.M. the show closes.

Once the cameras have stopped rolling, O. C. White walks over to me and says, "You know, there just might be something to what you said," and he walks away.

Memory Bank Activated: 5-27-1977
Content: The Choice to Make
Date: 1-1-1977 Time: 3:35 P.M.
Place: Apollo Village Apartment
Complex, Milwaukee, Wisconsin.

So this brings me back to the beginning of my story and how, on the first month, the first day of the year 1977, at 3:35 P.M., I had *my last* conversation with my Brother, Morris.

"Are you sure you want to go through with this?" Morris asked.

He didn't like the plan. "Look," he pointed out, "things are getting pretty hot over the music. A lot of people know you are the one responsible for putting this X-rated stuff on the market."

"Yeah, I know this." It was humorous to me.

"Some of the ones yelling the loudest are the ones that were part of the rip-off. Now they're coming back to me saying that the 'dog' they stole from me has bitten them."

"That's why I want to write this novel, to let the brothers and sisters in on some of the game they got waiting for them out here in this world. Sure, I formulated the songs with behavior-modifying words and concepts that were audio stimuli reinforcers, some positive and some negative. It will affect the population of this planet for generations to come. For those who promote, sell, and control this music, they will be putting themselves in the hands of the Angels, mentioned in Genesis 18:20-21."

Morris leaned back in his chair. "I'll admit it's changed quite a few ideologies. There's a lot of talk among the musicians who did your tunes. Many are professing a renewed faith in one form of religion or another and have started doing more relevant material."

"And some have gone in the opposite direction with it," I countered.

With local community organizations doing programs like Stopping Black-on-Black Crime and Unity in the Community, Morris tells me the elders think the positive "message music" will eclipse the negative effects of the sex records.

"They've even forecasted community self-control in the next few years for those cities with progressive Blacks living in them. Too bad I won't be here to see that." He sighed.

I bolted up off the couch! "Why… What's wrong?"

"Nothing," he reassured me. "It's just that I've got another assignment…in Africa. The Brothers over there are getting ready to make a historic move, and I'd like to be a part of it. The thought of living in a free Africa appeals to me."

"Sounds nice," I said. The idea intrigued me too. "If I became a freedom fighter, maybe get a guaranteed five hundred acres of land of my choice after the war for liberation was over…"

Morris threw up his hands, cutting me off. "See, there you go again; you've got to abandon that type of thinking! We've got a multitude of warriors! You're supposed to be one of the lovers of humanity that will help usher peace into the world. What's the Brotherhood verse you received from Master Seven?"

I recited the verse Master Seven had taught me. "Men seek to become gods, instead of seeking God. We can only come close to God when we live in Brotherhood, with love, and understanding between all people. That is walking the path of truth."

Morris smiled. "We've been on this journey together for over fifteen years, my Brother; that's a long time. I'm going to miss you. I don't agree with what you want to do.

Writing this book, I mean. But apparently, you have confidence that this is the right thing to do. I'll give your message to the elders about doing this thing. They will agree with me that this can only serve to put you out on front street and in harm's way; we've already lost enough people."

Then I saw a side of him I'd never seen before. Leaning forward, he said, "There's only a couple of us left who came up out of the 'Cobra's Den' in Chi-town." Getting to his feet, he prepared to leave. We gave each other the "dap" handshake used by 'Nam Vets, and I walked him out.

Closing the door behind him, I knew that a major part of my mission in life had come to an end, and I began to formulate this novel in my mind.

Memory Bank Activated: 5-28-1977
Subject: The Novel
Spy for Brotherhood No. 7
Content: Who Am I?
Memory Bank Information: Date: 1-7-1977
Time: 11:35 A.M.

On 1-7-1977 at 12:00 noon, I begin to meditate and study the data compiled. On 1-11-1977 at 12:10 P.M., I received a plain manilla envelope in the mail containing events that had been previously unknown to me. On 1-14-1977 at 7:07 A.M., after seven days of fasting, praying, and meditation, I began to draft this novel.

You may ask, *Who am I to write these things, and of what importance are they to you?* The story of our generation was foretold thousands of years ago by all the prophets. That periodically mankind will be heard as a collective voice crying unto God; Saying, Is it not the seventh year (Deuteronomy: Chapter 15:9)?

Beware that there be not a thought in thy wicked heart, saying the seventh year, the year of release is at hand; and thine eye be evil against thy poor brother and thou givest him naught, and he cries unto the Lord against thee, and it be sin unto thee.

Have not the "spokesmen" of God, Allah, the giver of enlightenment and teacher of divine reality said the same thing (SURA XLIX-Verse 10-The Holy Quran)?

The believers are but a single Brotherhood, so make peace and reconciliation between your two (contending) Brothers; and fear God, that ye may receive mercy.

Who am I to confront you with these things and tell you that the time of judgment is upon you? The time in man's existence when he teeters on the brink of salvation or self-destruction!

If ye live in peace, God shall truly walk upon the Earth once again! If ye advocate war and hate, then death shall be your fate.

Who am I to say these things?

Do you not know me?

I am the sleeper who has awakened. Born the second month on the day of the double sevens, In the year of the seven sevens.

Did they not tell you of my coming?

I am the Aquarian "Truth Seeker" who pours out ideas and is guarded by sword and shield.

The Dreamer of dreams that manifest into divine reality.

I am

The Invisible Man

Captain of the Mothership

Spy for Brotherhood!

B.E. Ware

COPYRIGHT 2022 ©